Treasure of the Apache

Tom Hyland

Published by Tom Hyland, 2022.

TREASURE OF THE APACHE

First edition. June 28, 2022.

Copyright © 2022 Tom Hyland.

ISBN: 979-8201328375

Written by Tom Hyland.

This Book is dedicated to
My Mom CINDY & My Dad MARK
who never cease to believe in me.
ALSO
To all the sources of inspiration during the writing
of this book whom I salute:
EDGAR RICE BURROUGHS,
L. RON HUBBARD,
ELMORE LEONARD,
BUDD BOETTICHER,
SAMUEL FULLER,
SERGIO LEONE,
SERGIO CORBUCCI,
SAM PECKINPAH,
MONTE HELLMAN,
TRAVIS MILLS,
GINA CARANO,
& Most Especially
DALLAS SONNIER

Special thanks to my beta readers and editors, especially Diane Surrusco for her input and to Gabriella West of *Edit for Indies* for her huge part in the editing of this novel.

2 TOM HYLAND

He knew he could not go much further. He staggered with each step that felt like a weight pulling him down. His body bled from the sweat of the desert and the wounds given to him from all the cacti along the way. His lips ached from the thirst that he could not quench. It was a hot day out in the middle of the desert of the Arizona Territory. Only a madman would be in a place like that, all alone, isolated, and completely exposed.

But he was an exception. He was a man on the run from his past and struggling for the present not to end him.

His name was Joel Macready. He was an older man in his late fifties with no gun, food, or water. The latter two he had run out of and the first he'd dumped a way's back so that he could travel with less weight on foot in the desert. His horse? It stepped into a prairie dog hole and broke its leg a few days back. He had to put it down after that. His only protection from the sun was a worn-out Stetson that didn't do much to protect him. Sweat poured down his face into his eyes, to add more discomfort to his sunburned face. For a moment he looked behind him as if he was expecting someone.

All he saw was the desert.

In front of him he was haunted by his little girl's face that he had abandoned thirteen years ago. It was in the blinding sun before him that the face hovered over him, the sweet face of his little girl. After he was a failure in Missouri, he came to the Arizona Territory with his wife and little girl.

The only problem was he carried his failure with him when he left Missouri behind. He'd tried his hands at everything—and he failed.

Eventually he found himself working as a ranch hand for rancher Rex Johnson in Border Town on the Arizona/New Mexico territorial line. His daughter found playmates in Rex's two young sons, and they embraced her like one of their own. One day his wife got scarlet fever and didn't recover.

He was devastated.

Feeling like he was unworthy to be a father, he left, returning to Missouri, leaving his daughter in the care of Rex Johnson. It was in Missouri that eventually the war broke out and he found himself drawn into it...

He shook his head.

"Don't think about it..."

All it did was make him more upset than he already was.

His heart pounded in his chest, ready to explode. Any minute, let alone a second, he would collapse and he knew it, but he pushed himself.

"Must keep going..."

He was a determined man.

"Must keep going... I must..."

There was still one more thing left that he had to do before he could die. He must set things right.

"Must..."

His aching legs finally began to give. He collapsed to his knees.

"Get up..."

He looked up into the blue Arizona sky. The buzzards were above him now, circling around him. Even they knew what was coming. He shook his head in stubborn defiance.

"No, not yet... Not yet..."

His knees cried as he tried to stand. Feeling the weight give away, he collapsed face down. The hot, reddish-brown sand scorched his face.

"Get..."

He could not stand. He was too weak. Too weak to even lift his head so that his face would not scorch against the hot sand. He began to cry, for he knew that he had failed the ultimate of tests.

He shut his eyes to keep the sand and dust from burning his sensitive eyes. All he could see was his little girl standing by the doorway as she was on the day he left, crying. She was crying for him not to go, for she did not want him to leave.

"I'm sorry... Jill, my girl... Please forgive me... I'm sorry... I'm sorry..."
Up above him the buzzards hovered over him, coming closer. It was only a matter of time before they would start to eat away at him.

While Joel Macready was preparing to meet his maker, a short distance away three riders in blue rode along. Three soldiers in blue. Two of them were green recruits, not even twenty years old. The third was in his late twenties and had the stripes of a sergeant.

It was the year 1865, one month after the end of the war between the states. The future of the Land of the Free was uncertain and its grand experiment was deemed a failure to the world all over. To Sergeant Ben Lobo, the real fighting was only beginning. Many alike from all over the war-torn South would begin the migration into the Western territories from New Mexico, Arizona, and the golden state of California to begin again. Lobo knew that would mean new settlements, but new settlements meant trouble with the Apaches. To a number of the California boys stationed at Fort Bowie who came on after Valverde and Apache Pass, that would be the end of their boredom, but to a hardened fighter like Lobo, it meant more blood.

That was something he had no intentions of sticking around for. The son of a white school teacher and a Vaquero ranch hand just outside of Santa Fe, there was little to offer a young man of mixed race in the West. The way he saw it, there were two choices for him:
Work as a ranch hand or become an outlaw.
Luckily for him a third option came along.
That was the Army.
The war between the states brought many young men calling up for the Army all over the territories to escape what little they had. What men like Lobo got was an extended stay at Fort Bowie to keep watch on the Union's interest in the West, but the Confederates did eventually arrive—and when they did come, they got hammered at Valverde, but

luckily there weren't that many of them in numbers, so the fighting more or less ceased after that, if you forgot a few guerrilla strikes here and there.

The main problem was not the Confederates, but the Apaches.

Carleton led them well against them at Apache Pass, but his methods were deemed extreme so he was eventually removed from command after the fighting was over. After Apache Pass the Apaches were rounded up and sent to San Carlos, or those lucky enough not to get caught escaped into the mountains where they pledged to fight on.

It was something of a waiting game from then on out after Valverde and Apache Pass.

However, those two battles were enough to tell Lobo that he was lucky he didn't get sent back East, where the stories and Union newspapers told them of the everyday carnage of fighting their brothers-in-arms, whereas Lobo only saw two major fights. One of them not even against the Confederates.

Two fights in four years was enough to last him a lifetime; but to have one practically every day, Lobo took his hat off to them. They had more guts than he ever did, as far as he was concerned.

So, what now?

For Ben Lobo he was calling it quits in the Army. He didn't know what he would do: probably work as a ranch hand like his father, or get a job as a Marshall in Santa Fe if they would have him. Four years in the military had humbled him, if anything, before his God, and taught him that some things you can only take what you can get out of life, because there are some things one is just not meant to have or do.

As for these California boys he knew like privates Steve Quinn and John Barton, with their eagerness of young cavaliers, Lobo knew that once they started fighting, they would only then wake up to the facts of life. They may have been on a routine patrol of the area, but listening to them talk of their eagerness for a fight made him think back as to how naïve he was when he first got into the Army. At the same time, he couldn't help, but miss what they were feeling and thinking. To him that was called innocence. The very thing he lost when he killed his first man on the battlefield at Valverde.

"I wonder what God was thinking when he made this territory," said Barton.

"Just what do ya mean by that?" asked Quinn, riding along next to him.

"I mean there's nothing and nobody out here."

"There's Apaches."

"Apaches," spat Barton. "Why, I haven't seen a single damn Apache since I got here. They've probably been gone since Carleton licked 'em at Apache Pass three years ago. Hell, it's bad enough that we ain't gonna get to kill any Johnny Rebs since they all called it quits last month at Appomattox."

"That figures," said Quinn. "All of us young bucks missed out on everything. My recruiter back home promised me an adventure in a wild land..."

"Wild, ha," laughed Barton. "The word I would have used is dead."

"Dead is sure a good way of putting it," said Quinn. "The only thing that seems to get by out here are the snakes and the coyotes. I don't see how an Apache can live out here."

"All right, you two, knock it off," ordered Lobo. "Let's just get this patrol over with so that we can get back to the damn garrison."

Who could blame Lobo right there? It was hot, with the sun at the highest point of the day, and they were wearing wool uniforms. The wool of the uniform wasn't made for comfort, but Lobo was used to it. The heat of Arizona was the same as it was in New Mexico. When you're born into it, it was easy to be used to it. To men like Quinn and Barton, who were used to the much more friendly California weather, it was a whole other beast to get used to.

They were about to turn back for the Fort when they spotted the buzzards up ahead just a mile off, encircling over a hill.

"What are those birds over there?" said Quinn upon spotting them. "They sure are moving in a suspicious pattern."

"They look like buzzards to me," said Barton.

"Buzzards?" said Quinn. "Don't they show up when something is dead?"

Lobo, sitting upon his horse, looked through his binoculars at the scene.

"They look like buzzards to me," repeated Barton.

"They are buzzards," confirmed Lobo, lowering his binoculars.

"Could that mean there's trouble?" asked Quinn.

"Apaches maybe," speculated Barton.

At the word Apaches both men got excited, eager for action, but Lobo was serious.

"Shut up," said bit Lobo. "We don't know what's over that hill. I need the two of ya to get serious right now.

"Yes, sir," said Barton.

"Yes, Sergeant," said Quinn.

"So, we check it out nice and easy-like," said Lobo. "All right, let's move."

At a trot they rode towards the scene. Once they got close to the hill they slowed their horses down a pace and proceeded up the hill with caution. They came to a stop up on the hill and looked out at the great divide.

Lobo scanned the scenery with his binoculars, looking at the scene for any sign or sight.

"See anything?" asked Barton.

"Can't see a thing out there," said Quinn.

"Wait a minute," said Lobo. "I see something."

"What is it?" asked Quinn.

"There's a man out there."

"A man?" retorted Barton.

"Yes," said Lobo. "He's lying face down in the sand."

The buzzards were starting to land on Macready to do their pickings as the three men in blue approached him. Lobo wasted no time taking out his Colt from his holster to fire a shot in the air to scare the birds away. Once they got to him, they quickly dismounted, and Lobo was the first to reach Macready's side.

Lobo gently lifted his face from the sand, turning him over towards him and checking his pulse on his neck.

"He's alive," said Lobo.

Lobo then began to shake him awake.

"Mister," urged Lobo. "Mister, come on, wake up."

Macready coughed into consciousness, sneezing from the sand that covered his face. He tried to speak.

"Don't speak," said Lobo. He turned to Barton. "Gimme yer canteen."

Barton handed Lobo his canteen, which he held up to the man's lips.

"Here," said Lobo. "Drink slowly."

The water was sweet to his lips. His body rejoiced at the taste of it.

"Can ya speak?" Lobo asked Macready.

"Yes," he said weakly.

"What's your name?"

"Joel Macready."

"Are there others?"

"No."

"Are the Apaches after ya?"

"No... I'm alone."

"Can ya stand?"

"I'll try."

"We're going to get ya to Fort Bowie, Mr. Macready," promised Lobo. "But I'm going to need you to take it slow and easy."

Lobo turned to the others.

"Help 'em onto the back of my horse," he ordered.

Quinn and Barton moved to help Macready up onto Lobo's horse. Lobo looked around with a sense of dread that they were being watched. By then Macready was up on Lobo's horse and Lobo sat behind Macready, taking the reins.

"Let's go," said Lobo.

All together they galloped away from the scene back to Fort Bowie.

Joel Macready may have been a man full of regret over his daughter, but he was also a liar about being alone.

About a mile behind where the army patrol found him, eight riders were galloping to catch up. They came to a stop at the sight of the Army patrol, which they saw approaching Macready in the distance.

The leader of the riders cursed at the sight of the patrol.

"Get outta sight," he ordered. "Behind 'em rocks."

They did as their leader said hid behind some rocks with their horses. Their leader was as tall as a mountain with a baby face and piercing blue eyes. His name was Charlie St. Luc and he had the look of a killer. He took out a scope and watched the scene play out before him with a keen eye.

The others with him were determined underlings that were as weary of the chase as he was and eager for the kill and the big payoff to come. Their second in command and the smartest one outside of Charlie was Sugar Lee. The others consisted of Silent Duke, who was a six-foot-two Texan that never spoke much and could easily be mistaken for a mute, and Killer Bill Cody, the meanest of the bunch, who used his Bowie knife for scalping people just for the hell of it. One-Eyed Jack was the sharpshooter, but was blind in his left eye and wore an eye patch over it. Doc Smith was the doctor among them, but his main specialty was dentistry. Then there was Buckshot Joe, whose weapon of choice was a shotgun. Last but not least was Kid Gray, the youngest one and the dumbest of them all. He was the wild card.

Their age ranges were diverse, but they all had one thing in common.

They were killers.

"What is it, boss?" asked Sugar Lee.

"Army patrol," said Charlie.

"There's only three of 'em, boss," said Kid Gray anxiously. "Why don't we take 'em?"

Charlie looked away at the scope to the Kid with a rough look on his face. A look that said he didn't have the patience or grit to put up with simple stupidity.

"Do you know where we are, Kid?" he asked him.

"The middle of the desert," said Kid Gray, confused.

"Do you know where in the desert?" said Charlie.

"Uh, no..."

"If you see an Army patrol, Kid, what does that mean?" Charlie asked him seriously.

The Kid hesitated and began to tremble in his boots from the pressure. Sugar Lee saw that he was getting to the Kid and decided to answer for him.

"That means there's a whole garrison of Yankees nearby," he said.

Charlie quickly turned to Sugar Lee and gave him a look of instant approval, completely forgetting about the Kid.

"Exactly," said Charlie.

Kid Gray still didn't get it and dumbly opened his mouth, at which point Sugar Lee shook his head and gave up on helping him out.

"But there's just three of 'em," said Kid Gray. "We can lick three like easy."

This time Charlie lost his cool.

"You damn halfwit," he snapped. "Do ya want an entire Yankee garrison down our throats? We're almost out of water. Horses won't last without water."

Kid Gray backed down, shaking in his boots, finally getting the message. Sometimes it took a little confrontation to get through to him.

"Sorry, boss."

"Sorry ain't gonna' cut it, Kid," bit Charlie. "Use your noggin'!"

"But what are we gonna' do?" said a frustrated Doc Smith. "We just can't let the Army take 'em."

"We're not screwed yet, boys."

"But how?" said One-Eyed Jack. "The damn Yankees just got 'em."

Charlie shook his head in frustration at his men's stupidity. Sometimes he just wanted to put an end to them all and just start over, either on his own or with just Sugar Lee.

"He can't ask for protection, otherwise they'd slap chains on 'em," said Charlie. "No, he'll be forced to move on. This'll give us some time to rest and water our horses. If there's a garrison nearby then there must be a stagecoach or mailing station too. We'll stay close to there. His horse died on him a few days ago and the Army isn't in the business of just handing out horses like some Church charity. We woulda won the war easy if they were."

"No, sir," added Sugar Lee. "He'll be forced to take the coach, which'll be easy for us to take."

"That's right," smiled Buckshot Joe.

"We'll take our time following 'em, boys," said Charlie, looking through the scope. "They're out of sight. Come on. Let's get back on the horses."

They got up from behind the rocks and headed up on their horses. Before Charlie could get on his horse Killer Bill walked right up behind him and spoke to him in a menacing tone, which forced Charlie to freeze.

"Even if we catch up to 'em, we know he don't have the goods on 'em," said Killer Bill. "We know he hid it back in Apache Territory..."

"What's yer point, Bill?" said Charlie.

"My point is, he'll die before he'll tell us," said Killer Bill, raising his voice. "I said it before, you were soft on him on account..."

Charlie stopped him cold with a sinister voice that Killer Bill recognized all too well.

"On account of what, Bill?"

Killer Bill hesitated. It was his turn to shake in his boots.

"Go on," said Charlie. "You were obviously about to state something important to ya."

Killer Bill was dead silent.

"Oh, so you were finished," said Charlie. "Well, allow me to respond in kind..."

Suddenly Charlie turned around and swung his fist into Killer Bill's face, knocking him on the ground. He landed on his back, getting the wind knocked out of him, and he went for his Bowie knife, but Charlie already had his gun on him and his boot against his chest. Killer Bill lay there looking up at him with a look of cold, naked fear.

His hand remained on his knife in its sheath.

"Go ahead, Bill," dared Charlie. "Pull yer toothpick on me. See how far you'll get with trying to scalp me before I blow yer damn head clean off!"

Killer Bill continued to hesitate. He just lay there.

"Go ahead!" said Charlie with a crazed look on his face. "Pull it!"

Slowly, Killer Bill took his hand off of his knife and slowly put his hands out to where Charlie could see them. He was smart enough to know that this was one fight he didn't stand a chance in hell of surviving.

"That's what I thought," said Charlie.

He got his boot off Killer Bill and holstered his gun. Killer Bill quickly got up and onto his horse. Charlie, meanwhile, looked around and saw that everyone was looking at him.

"Joel didn't just fool me," said Charlie. "He fooled all of us. He stole what was ours and kept it for himself. That's why we're goin' to catch 'em and take back what is rightfully ours in the eyes of God himself!"

"Then we kill 'em," smiled Kid Gray.

Charlie looked to Kid Gray. He didn't give him a condescending look, but the look of one looking at a child.

"Kill him?" said Charlie. "No, he'll die alright, but killing would be too easy for him. And believe me, boys, we ain't gonna' make it easy for 'em one damn bit."

It was a twenty-minute ride back to Fort Bowie. The army outpost consisted of a fort barracks surrounded by walls, with a guard post to keep an eye out for danger. The guard at the gate immediately spotted them as they approached.

"Open the gate," ordered Lobo upon approaching. "Fetch Doc."

The guard at the guard posted orders to open the gate. Soldiers scrambled to open the gate to allow them to enter. All hands rushed to assist the three riders, including Captain Harry Sheldon, who approached Lobo's horse with two privates to help Macready down.

Like Ben Lobo, Harry Sheldon was a veteran of Valverde and Apache Pass, but he was a few years older than Lobo and in the Army a few years longer. Harry Sheldon was a thirty-two-year-old, six-foot-tall man of half white and half Black heritage, but was fair-skinned enough to pass as a white.

The white part of him alone was what got him into West Point back in the mid-1850s. Like Lobo, he was from the New Mexico Territory, but he was the son of a blacksmith and a Black Baptist preacher's daughter.

"What happened, Sergeant?" Sheldon asked Lobo.

"We found 'em lying face down in the sand about five miles from here," answered Lobo. "He was all alone with no horse or nothing on 'em."

"Did he say anything?"

By then the two privates had gotten Macready off Lobo's horse and taken him into the barracks to the doctor.

"Nothing really, except that he's alone and no one's after 'em," said Lobo.

"But judging by the look on yer face, you don't believe him," said Sheldon.

"Something's off," said Lobo. "I dunno what, but..."

"You got a feeling," said Sheldon. "I've known you long enough to take those serious. All three of you report to Colonel Harding right away."

All three men replied with a "yes, sir" and salute before getting off their horses. They handed their horses off to the sergeant at the stable before heading into Colonel Harding's office. Already Sheldon was there, giving his version of the story.

"...Judging by the situation, I suggest, with the Colonel's permission, that we put the garrison on alert and..."

He stopped when Lobo, Barton, and Quinn entered to remove their hats and salute in their full attention.

"At ease..." said Harding. "Report, Sergeant. Who is this man?"

"He identified himself as a Joel Macready, sir," said Lobo. "He said he was alone."

"But ya don't think so?" said Harding.

"Well, sir," said Lobo, "I got the impression that he was running from someone or..."

"...Something," finished Harding.

"Yes, sir," said Lobo.

"I see," said Harding. "What was he carrying?"

"Nothing but the clothes on his back," answered Lobo.

"No gun?"

"No, sir," said Lobo. "Not even a canteen."

"What do ya suggest we do?" said Harding.

"Well, sir," said Lobo, "for starters, I'd say put the garrison on alert and send out more patrols to scout the area to be sure he really wasn't alone."

"All right," said Harding. He turned to Sheldon. "Harry, I'm putting you in charge of that."

"Yes, sir," said Sheldon.

"Proceed," said Harding.

"Yes, sir," said Sheldon.

With nothing else said, Captain Sheldon left to carry out his orders. Once he was gone Harding turned his attention directly to Ben Lobo.

"Here's the thing, Sergeant," said Harding. "This past year we've had many men from the South come through here. Some of 'em are deserters, while others are trying to get to family that have settled out here. Now that the war is over more of 'em'll be coming. Some will be seeking a new start while others will be trouble. It might be a strain on Indian relations. You're not gonna be here, which may be the smart thing; besides, you've earned your spurs between Valverde and Apache Pass. Hell, ya were decorated for your gallantry. Now as far as Macready goes, there won't be a whole lot we can do. If he asks for help or if he doesn't answer our questions properly, then we'll be able to do something. If he's well enough to travel, we'll pay for his ticket for the coach and that's all we'll do."

There was a knock at the door.

"Yes, come in," called Harding.

The garrison doctor, Lou McCoy, entered to give a report of his examination of Macready.

"Yes, Lou," said Harding. "What's your prognosis?"

"He'll live," said McCoy. "He was just dehydrated from a long journey."

"Did he say anything?"

"Oh, nothing much," said McCoy. "He's just trying to get to his daughter out on Border Town."

"The New Mexico-Arizona territorial line? That Border Town?"

"I can't think of any other," said McCoy.

"What's he doing now?"

"Right now, he's getting himself a shave and a much-needed bath," said McCoy. "After that he'll get something to eat."

"When can we talk to him?" asked Harding.

"Well, this evening, I suppose, after he's rested a bit."

"He'll be staying, then?" said Harding.

"Just for two days to get on the coach to Contention," said McCoy. "From there he'll get to Border Town."

"If that's where he's going," said Harding.

"Oh, I'd say he's telling the truth on that end, at least," said McCoy.

"What makes ya say that?"

"Because he is a man that has lost everything that mattered to him and then some, or he didn't realize it until it was too late."

"Did he give you a sob story?"

"He didn't have to," said McCoy. "It was written all over his face."

"I see," said Harding. "All right, Lou. Keep an eye on 'em."

"I will," said McCoy.

McCoy excused himself. Harding then looked to Lobo, Barton, and Quinn.

"All right," said Harding, "until I've had a word with 'em I don't want 'em wandering around the Fort."

"I agree," said Lobo.

"Keep 'em confined to his quarters until he leaves," said Harding.

"Yes, sir," said Lobo.

"Dismissed."

The eight riders that consisted of the St. Luc gang rode into the Butter
Land Overland Mail station at Apache Pass near the Fort later that day.
The place wasn't much, just a small outpost for the stagecoach. Next
door stood an adobe building that had the word SALOON printed on
front. Right out front was a railing for the horses to be tied down.

The gang came to a stop at the railing and dismounted to tie their
horses up before entering the narrow saloon. The interior had a
mahogany bar and on the opposite sides f the door was a long plank
table with eight Douglas chairs. One could sit to eat and drink.
Between the bar and the table was a roll-up desk. The saloon keeper,
Carlos, ran it alone. Upon the gang's entry, Carlos, a short, balding
Mexican, was quick to see that these men could be trouble. But
nonetheless, he decided to play it cool.

Be friendly.

Be himself.

"*Hola, senors,*" he greeted them. "Good to see you."

Kid Gray instantly took offense to the friendly Mexican speaking
to him. He never wanted to waste a moment speaking to peons, which
to him Carlos was.

"How would ya know, ya damn greaser?" he spat. "Ya ain't seen us
before... or have ya?"

Carlos was instantly startled. For a second, he thought he was going
to get killed, but Sugar Lee, who happened to be the nearest person to
the Kid, yanked him back a foot by the shoulder.

"Shut up, ya fool," snapped Sugar Lee.

Charlie saw that the situation could get worse and stepped right in
between Kid Gray and Carlos at the bar to look at the Mexican almost
friendly.

"Ya have to forgive the Kid," said Charlie. "He's more
even-tempered on a good day. Besides, it's been a long ride for us to get
to this point."

Carlos relaxed and decided to go with the flow of it.

"That is okay, senor," he said. "I quite understand. There's a lot of people coming through here after the war these days. What can I get you?"

"Whiskey for each of us, please," said Charlie.

"Just sit yourselves down at the bar," said Carlos. "I'll give each of you a glass."

"Leave the bottle for us, please," said Charlie.

"*Si, senor*," agreed Carlos. "I can do that. I can fix you and your *amigos* some beans, if you like."

All the men sat at the bar. Charlie responded in kind to Carlos's offer.

"We would love to have something to eat," said Charlie. "We haven't eaten all day."

Carlos served them their drinks.

"*Si, senor*," said Carlos. "I will just go back and begin cooking. I'll be a few minutes."

"We got all the time in the world," said Charlie. "Thank you."

By then Carlos had finished serving them their drinks and left them the bottle before leaving out back to begin cooking. Once he was out of sight, Charlie changed his friendly demeanor and turned his anger back to Kid Gray once again.

"Do I have to lecture ya on the meaning of the word inconspicuous?" said Charlie.

"Inca-Pious?" said Kid Gray, not getting the word. "What now?"

"Okay," said Charlie sarcastically. "Let me sound it out for ya so that yer simpleton mind can grasp the word. In-Con-Spic-U-Ous. It means not staying visible or attracting attention. What ya did just now was the opposite of what we're trying to go for."

"What the fuck did I just do?" said Kid Gray defensively.

"Pick a pissing contest with that greaser for starters," said Sugar Lee.

"Shut up, Sugar," bit Charlie. "I'll explain it this time."

"Wait," said Kid Gray. "You're sore over the way I spoke to that nosy Mexican? I've said worse to people."

That statement alone got some laughs from the men, but not Charlie.

"Listen to me, Kid, and this goes for the rest of all of y'all, so all y'all listen," said Charlie. "If those Yankees at that Fort, wherever it is, are smart, which I'm betting my chips they are, they will be on the lookout for any suspicious characters, and that includes outsiders—."

"So what?" said Kid Gray. "Ya said it yourself that if Joel is smart, he won't say anything if he wants..."

"Damn it, Kid, if you were them, would you take his story at face value?" bit Charlie. "After all this country has been through, do you think they're going to take any chances?"

That's when it all began to finally sink in to Kid Gray. He just sat there dumbfounded with his mouth wide open.

"Now, you use yer head," said Charlie. "Thank ya. It's good to know that ya can be useful with your head along with the gun."

"What are we supposed to do, boss?" asked Kid Gray.

"Just relax and don't say anything that'll make anyone suspicious," said Charlie. "That goes for the rest of you as well."

"Like what?" asked Kid Gray his mouth japed.

"How the hell do I know?" snapped Charlie. "Just keep yer damn mouth shut. You never say anything useful with it anyway."

That got some laughs from the men. Before Kid Gray could respond three soldiers entered the saloon and everyone went deathly silent. One of the soldiers was Sergeant Mark "Sully" Sullivan, another veteran of Valverde and Apache Pass. The other two were freshly green recruits that came on around the same time as Barton and Quinn, both of them buck privates. Slowly, they approached the St. Luc gang. All three of them were armed.

The gang pretended to go about their business while the soldiers made their approach. Charlie himself turned around when they got behind him two to three feet away.

"Afternoon, gentlemen," Charlie greeted.

"Afternoon, gentlemen," Sully greeted back. "Y'all passing through?"

"Yes, sir," said Charlie with a smile. "On our way to California. We've heard that's where things are happening."

"Yes, things are happening out that way," agreed Sully. "Is this all of you?"

"Why, yes," said Charlie. "Is there something wrong?"

"No, no, nothing like that," insisted Sully. "It's just that we found a fellow out in the desert on his own today and we're trying to find out if he was with anybody."

"Not with us," said Charlie. "It's just us eight. Did he say he was with somebody?"

"No, no," said Sully. "Not specifically, but given the situation and the fact that this is Apache country, it helps to know all you can."

"I couldn't agree with ya more," said Charlie. "It's always good to know everything, because ya never know what surprises may pop up."

Sully laughed.

"Yes, that's true," he agreed. "Say, where did you say ya guys were from?"

"We didn't," said Charlie.

"Oh, well I guess ya didn't," said Sully. "So...?"

"So, what?" said Charlie.

"Where y'all from?"

"Oh, we all hail from Kansas City," said Charlie.

"That in Missouri?"

"The same."

"Rough time in Missouri, so I heard."

"Yes, so it was."

"Done any fighting?"

"We did our part."

"Yeah, we did our part out here as well," said Sully.

"Valverde?" asked Charlie.

"Along with a few dust-ups with the Apaches."

"How are the Apaches at this time of the year?"

"There are only two kinds of Apaches in this Territory, friend," said Sully. "Wild and contained at San Carlos or wild and free in the mountains. Not too many white men wander up those parts unless they got themselves a death wish."

"On account of 'em bein' savages," said Kid Gray, opening his mouth.

Sully looked at Kid Gray. Charlie meanwhile gives him a look out of Sully's eyeshot that says careful.

"On account of 'em being wounded and against the wall," said Sully. "You see, there's nothing more dangerous than a wounded man with his back against the wall. The kind of man that had everything and everyone he knew taken away from him. Losing does something to you. It creates a sort of catharsis that can bring about the worst in 'em..."

"You talk as though the savage were a man," said Sugar Lee. "Anyone that lives like an animal is nothing more than a heathen."

"That depends on how you look at it, friend," said Sully.

"You see, where we come from, a man ain't somethin' unless he's willin' to fight for what's his," said Sugar Lee.

"What makes you think that the Apaches are no different than, let's say, a Johnny Reb?" said Sully. "They're both fighters who fought for what's theirs."

"Except they both lost and your side won on both fronts," said Charlie. "Where does that leave 'em? What do they do then? Do they fight on or move on?"

"I guess I'm not the right person to answer that," said Sully. "I don't know what it's like to lose, but you do. Don't ya?"

Charlie stared at him for a moment before answering.

"Yes, we do," he answered.

That was when an understanding came to Sully as he looked at Charlie and each of his men. It was an understanding that this was a fight that he would lose if he chose to fight it. Sometimes it was best to let a dog lie.

"Well, good luck to y'all," said Sully politely.

"And to you," said Charlie.

Sully and his two men turned around and left the saloon. All eyes then turned to Charlie while he turned to look in front of him.

"What was that all about?" said One-Eyed Jack.

"He was just feelin' us out," said Charlie. "All we did was tell him that we're not to be trifled with."

"You say to play it cool and what do you do?" jumped One-Eyed Jack. "Ya play around with him, ya, the Kid, and Sugar."

"He would have sniffed us out whether we said somethin' or not," said Sugar Lee.

"Oh, and how do you know that?" said One-Eyed Jack.

"Jack, any man who has had a taste of war can scent it out on anyone," said Charlie. "All we did was make sure that he would think twice before bein' nosy any further."

"And what if he's not smart enough to think about it?" said One-Eyed Jack.

Before Charlie could answer Carlos came out with some bowls to give each of them.

"It's almost done, *senors*," said Carlos. "I'll be just another minute or two."

"Say, ya wouldn't happen to know when the next stage will be arriving, do you?" asked Charlie.

"Two days from now, *senor*," answered Carlos. "It should be here by, oh, I'd say noon. No later than that."

"Good to know," said Charlie. "Thank ya kindly."

"*De nada, senor*," said Carlos graciously. "*De nada.*"

Carlos went back to the kitchen to check on the food, leaving Charlie and his gang alone for another moment.

"Boys," said Charlie. "Joel will be on that stage. That I am most certain about."

"What's the play, boss?" asked Kid Gray.

"We eat," said Charlie. "Afterwards, we water and resupply ourselves and our horses. Then we make camp some ways from here, close enough to get a good eye on this place. Once he's aboard we'll follow them a ways away from this place and ambush 'em."

"What if he doesn't talk though, boss?" said One-Eyed Jack. "If I were in his shoes I'd tell y'all to go to Hell in a hand basket."

"Very true," said Charlie. "I agree with you there. That's why we'll use his daughter against him."

"Daughter?" said Kid Gray. "Joel's got a daughter?"

"This is first we're hearin' about this," said Doc Smith.

"Well, he told me private-like that he's got one," said Charlie. "From what I gather, he abandoned her over a decade ago, and last he heard she was living in some place called Border Town. We threaten Joel with his daughter's life, then he might budge a thing or two. Plus, knowin' Joel, he wrote a map to where he put the gold, no doubt. If he doesn't have it on 'em, the chances are, he had it sent to her. All we'd have to do is pay her a visit."

"But we're goin' to pay her a visit anyways," said Kid Gray playfully.

"Of course we are," said Charlie with a smile. "I'm curious as to how Joel Macready's daughter turned out. She might be a bit spirited for our amusement."

"Amen to that," laughed Kid Gray.

A moment later Carlos came out with their food and they ate in silence.

After Macready shaved, bathed, and put some beans and coffee in his belly he sat on his bed, still worn out. He was worn out from years of guilt and regret. Even when he was all cleaned up, he looked much older than his age. Some might say he looked somewhat like old Robert E. Lee, but much worse than he did the day he surrendered to Grant. Years of regret will age you pretty badly.

Like what Charlie had said, Macready had written out a map to where he hid what he took from them. He still had it with him, which was with a letter he had written to his daughter. Right then he was in a dilemma. Should he hold onto the letter and map and give it to her himself, but risk the chance of Charlie St. Luc and his gang getting their hands on it should they catch him before he gets to her? Or should he give it to someone else to send it and go off in a different direction to lead the gang on a wild goose chase? That would buy his daughter some time to go recover the gold for herself should she decide to take it. But what if she wasn't alive?

No, he reasoned. He knew she was alive. If she wasn't, then he would have felt it. She was not only alive, but she was at Rex Johnson's place where he'd raised her as his own. The latter alternative would probably be his only option to ensure it got to her, but he really wanted to face her himself.

But could he?

How could he face her after all these years? What did he have to show for his time away from her? All he had to show was more failure and four years mixing with bad company during a war that he should not have been there to fight in the first place.

While he was deep in thought over the matter there was a knock at the door.

"Come in," said Macready.

Colonel Harding entered. Macready stood up to receive him.

"No, no, please don't stand," said Harding. "Please sit, Mr. Macready."

Macready sat down. Harding stood.

"That's kind of you," said Macready.

"I'm Colonel Harding, Mr. Macready," said Harding. "Do ya mind if I sit with ya?"

"By all means, please do."

Harding sat down on the bed next to him.

"I'm pleased to meet you, Colonel," said Macready, attempting to be formal.

"Likewise, Mr. Macready," said Harding. "I just have a few questions for ya if ya don't mind."

"Ask away," said Macready.

"It's just a routine formality," said Harding. "That's all since the war's over and this being Apache Territory. We just have to be sure."

"I see."

"The first question I got to ask is what were you doing out there? Didn't you have a horse?"

"I did," said Macready. "It died on me about, oh I'd say two days ago. I had to put it down due to a broken leg. From there I was on foot."

"And you were traveling alone?"

"Yes, I was."

"I see," said Harding. "Where were you originally headed before you ended up here if you don't mind me asking?"

"I was or I am going to Border Town."

"Do you have relations there?"

"My daughter."

"Go on."

Macready was starting to feel uneasy and Harding could see it. He could even see if the man was hiding a few things from him, which he suspected he was. This was a man filled with regret like what Doc McCoy said. Traces of tears were beginning to appear on Macready's face.

"After her mother died, I didn't think I had it in me to raise a little girl alone as a ranch hand," said Macready. "So, I left her in the care of this rancher that I was working for and I went back to Missouri. It wasn't easy, but I just didn't know what else I could have done for her. I planned on coming back. Really, I did, but then the war broke out and..."

"I see," said Harding, getting the picture. "From what I read things were pretty rough in Missouri. Where in Missouri?"

"Kansas City."

He didn't ask him which side he was on, but if he was in Missouri, Harding figured he must have fought for the losing side of the war. There was nothing else he had to ask him. What else could he ask him?

With nothing else to say he excused himself and left Macready alone to his thoughts. Upon exiting, he spotted Sergeants Lobo and Sullivan at the stable, talking. Harding realized that Sully had just returned from a patrol.

He was very interested in what he had to say. Upon approaching them, they stood at attention to salute.

"At ease," said Harding. "Report, Sully."

"There are eight men at Carlos's saloon. Not your regular rebel types."

"How so?" asked Harding.

"Kansas City."

That got Harding's attention instantly. He did not believe in coincidence.

"Really," said Harding. "That was where Quantrill and his bunch roamed. I talked to our guest."

"What did he say?" asked Lobo.

"Well, for starters, he too is from Kansas City."

That sparked Lobo's interest as well.

"What else?" asked Lobo.

"Just like what Doc McCoy said. He's a broken man. I believe that. As far as getting the whole story, that's something else entirely, I suspect."

"What about these new guys?" said Lobo. "What if they're after him?"

"Then they'll be moving on from here," said Harding. "That's what I care about. If Macready wants our help, he'll have to say so. Otherwise the Army will not interfere."

"When will he be leaving?" asked Lobo.

"He'll be on the stage to Contention in two days," said Harding. "I'll see to that."

"They could jump him on the stage," said Lobo.

"I've thought about that so I've made a decision," said Harding. "This stage will have a three-man escort straight to Contention. Ben, I'd pick ya to lead it, but yer commission ends in three days and you'll be far away from here after that... Oh, have Sergeant Parker and two volunteers go..."

"Permission to speak freely, sir," said Lobo.

"Granted."

"If these men hail from Kansas City, then it'll take more than three men to stand up to 'em. Let alone a man like Sergeant Parker. He lacks the field experience."

"What do ya suggest?" asked Harding.

"Six men," said Lobo. "Each of them with fighting experience."

"I must agree with Sergeant Lobo, sir," said Sully. "These guys are not to be trifled with by men with a lack of field experience."

"I can't afford to spare that many men for a menial task," said Harding. "Let alone experienced men. It's bad enough we're losing you, Ben. With the war over a lot of people are going to be coming here. That might stir things up a bit with the Apaches, or it might not. I dunno. Whatever the case, I can't spare them. Hell, it might not be anything at all. When they get into Contention, they'll wire back to the Fort."

"And if they don't?" said Lobo.

"Then the message will be received," said Harding. "Something went wrong."

Harding walked away, leaving Lobo and Sully alone. Sully looked uneasy about the whole thing, but Lobo, on the other hand, despite being uneasy, understood where the Colonel was coming from.

"I don't like it, Ben," said Sully.

"Ya can't blame the Colonel for his decision," said Lobo. "In a way, he's right."

"What in the Hell makes ya say that?"

"Why do ya think I'm leaving, Sully?" said Lobo. "The war may be over, but the fight to tame this land will happen soon. When it does a whole lot of people will die in the crosshairs. I don't want to be in the crosshairs. I don't plan on being in the middle."

"Ya didn't see those eight fellows in Carlos's place," said Sully. "They're armed to the teeth and from what I got out of them if you're in their way, ya better stay out of it. Parker won't stand a chance against 'em."

"That's if they're after the guy."

"Today we have encountered nine strangers," said Sully. "One on his own and eight, close behind. All of them hail from Kansas City. I don't buy it that they don't know each other."

"Frankly, neither do I," said Lobo, "but what can we do? Really, what can we do?"

Sully was quiet for a moment. He knew that there was not a thing that he could do about it as much as Lobo could.

"You're right, I suppose," said Sully. "But damn it, man, it isn't right."

"What has been right about these past four years?" said Lobo. "How many lives did we take?"

"That was war."

"True," said Lobo, "but the way I see it, there's going to be a whole lot more of that coming this way, and I don't plan on being here for it."

"Had your bellyful, huh?"

"Yeah, ya could say that."

"Where will ya go?"

"Anyplace but here," said Lobo. "Maybe back to Santa Fe. Maybe head down to the Pacific. I don't know."

Two days passed without incident. The St. Luc gang vanished from the saloon, disappearing into the nearby hills to make camp to await the stage. Ben Lobo was given a day of leave, which he spent at the Butterfield mail station, the only place outside the Fort to be. Lobo, like every other soldier, did not spend his leave there, but in Carlos's saloon next door.

When Lobo walked into the saloon, he found that he wasn't alone. Inside, sitting in the middle chair, was Captain Harry Sheldon himself. Carlos was nearby cleaning a few glasses when Lobo stepped inside.

He was instantly greeted.

"*Hola, senor* Lobo," called Carlos. "I see you have your leave—and only a day before your commission's end, eh?"

"That's right, Carlos," nodded Lobo. "Ya remember the days well."

"What will it be?"

"Oh, I guess I'll have mescal," said Lobo.

"*Si, senor.*"

Lobo walked up to the gallant captain and sat on the stool next to him.

"Mind if I join ya, Captain?"

"Certainly, Sergeant," said Sheldon. "Or should I say Mr. Lobo?"

"Not for another day," said Lobo. "For the rest of the day it's still Sergeant."

"It doesn't have to be with me," smiled Luck. "You've earned your spurs. God knows it."

"I happen to agree with the Captain, senor Lobo," said Carlos putting a bottle of mescal before the soon-to-be-decommissioned Sergeant. "As for these California boys that come in, it'll take some time to get used to them. They prefer whiskey to the mescal, but we're on short supply of whiskey compared to mescal."

"They'll learn to love it," said Sheldon. "Don't ya worry about that, Carlos."

"*Si, senor.*"

There was always something to do in the Army. If you were not kept busy, you drank. That was about all Lobo or any fellow soldier on leave could do.

Word of Macready's rescue had reached the saloon, and it was not long before Carlos tried to get some information out of Lobo.

"Word was it that it was you who found a man out in the desert, senor Lobo," said Carlos.

"That's right," said Lobo between sips.

"Word also has it that he's got a peculiar story."

"What do you mean, peculiar?" said Lobo.

"Well, I mean, man says he's riding out to Contention on a horse. Somehow it dies and he winds up here. I mean, that doesn't sound like a real convincing story."

"You know what I think, Carlos," said Lobo. "I think you get pretty bored running this place that all ya can do is come up with stories out of the latest gossip."

"Senor, there's no need to get cranky with me. I was just stating my opinion."

"Then don't."

"The senor doesn't care?"

"Yes, the senor doesn't care," quipped Lobo.

Sheldon meanwhile sat there laughing.

"Carlos," continued Lobo, "I spent all day today signing my release papers and I should be getting on that coach coming in today. Instead, I gotta ride it out here tomorrow on a horse in this heat to Contention so that I can catch a coach to... Oh, why am I going on to ya about all this?"

"That's because you're homesick," teased Sheldon.

"*Si*," laughed Carlos. "The senor is a little homesick."

"Yeah," said Lobo sarcastically, "for Santa Fe."

"Okay, senor," said Carlos, still laughing. "Whatever makes you feel better."

Carlos walked away to get back to his cleaning, leaving Sheldon and Lobo to talk amongst themselves.

"So, *Sergeant*," began Sheldon, "word has it you're going back to Santa Fe."

"Maybe," said Lobo. "Maybe not. I haven't decided yet."

"Ya could always stay in the Army."

"Oh, no," shook Lobo. "I'm not doing that. Ya know it as much as I do that the fighting is only getting started out here with the Apaches. Plus, a lot of people will be migrating here from the war-torn South. That's going to be a lot of trouble for you, Captain."

"I don't see why you don't stay," said Sheldon. "The Army provided well for you."

"Yeah, well I don't think it's the life for me any longer."

"You and I both practically come from similar circumstances," said Sheldon. "We're both the offspring of mixed marriages. Our families were practically poor..."

"Let me stop you right there before ya dwell any further on the subject, Captain," said Lobo, raising his hand. "Otherwise I'm only going to get ornery with you, and I respect you too much to want to do that. You're an officer. I'm not. Period."

"You can always be one yourself," said Sheldon. "You got the chops of one."

"Maybe, but unlike you I'm not a West Pointer," said Lobo. "Sure, your mother was Black, but you can actually pass as a white in most places. Close enough to have gotten into West Point. I'm not on the fair-skinned side like you. There are some parts of this Territory alone that I wouldn't dare venture into. I'm not trying to bring you down, Captain. I'm just being realistic. A Mexican isn't considered an equal to a white man. Sure, you can say the same about the Blacks, but the Lord gave you a much fairer color to blend in better than he did with me. No, I'll have to take what I can get. Chances are, I'll either go back to working as a ranch hand like my father did or go into law enforcement. Probably the latter."

Sheldon wasn't going to argue with him. He knew he was right. They may have been dealt by the same dealer, but that didn't mean their cards would be the same.

"Okay," said Sheldon. "You may be right about where you came from, but that doesn't mean it doesn't define you."

"What do you mean by that?"

"I mean you can decide for yourself what it is that you want to be," said Sheldon. "But if you limit yourself to what everybody says you should be, then you won't be much of anybody. If you want something, then go for it. Don't sit back and wait for somebody else's scraps. It's not worth it."

Ben Lobo looked at the man who was a few years older than he was. They both had about the same fighting experience, but there was a big difference between them.

"You already know what you want," said Lobo. "I haven't yet figured out what it is that I want."

Harry Sheldon smiled at him. It was the smile one gives a kid brother.

"Well, when you do," said Sheldon. "Don't pass it up for the easy way through life. You'll only regret it in the end."

"You sound like you speak from experience."

"My father limited himself to what he could do," said Sheldon. "From a young age he told me to never make the same mistake he did. I took his advice. Advice is all that I'm offering ya, Sergeant."

Lobo smiled. He appreciated the man's advice. He really did. No one ever stopped to even do the same. Ever.

"You take care of yourself, Captain," said Lobo, "wherever the Army leads you."

"And you do the same, Sergeant," said Sheldon, "wherever life leads you."

Sheldon laid some money on the counter and nodded to Carlos.

"I'll see you later, Carlos," he said.

"Si, senor Sheldon," said Carlos, walking over to collect the money. "See you next time."

"I'll see you in the morning before you go, Sergeant," said Sheldon.

"See you then," acknowledged Lobo.

Without saying another word, Captain Harry Sheldon grabbed his officer's Stetson sitting on the stool next to him and walked out, putting it on.

Sitting alone, Carlos walked up to Lobo to offer him a piece of his mind.

"It's not as bad as you make it out to be, senor Lobo," said Carlos.

"You offering yer piece of mind as well, Carlos?" said Lobo cordially.

"If you don't mind then, yes."

"Go ahead," said Lobo. "I'm listening."

"My father, he was a horse thief," began Carlos. "They hanged him when I was a little boy. My mother, she died when I was thirteen. Ever since then I've been working. I worked whatever job I could get whether it be cattle drives, ranch hands, you name it. And I was frustrated, senor. I work so hard and get so little in return, but then one day eight years ago before you arrived I got a job at this saloon for old man Boone. He died two years later leaving no family behind, very sad.

The day after the funeral I was told that he left this place to me. At first, I was like, what am I going to do running a saloon? Then something occurred to me. I said, Carlos, this just might be a chance for you to have some stability for once in your life, so take it. I have not looked back ever since. Is it, hard work? Yes, it is, but I wake up every morning knowing that this business is mine. I own it. I feed the bellies of the Yankee soldiers and parch their thirst for mescal or whiskey. One day maybe when civilization comes to the Territory and the Territory joins the Union, then maybe I'll go out of business. But Carlos, he saves and he scrimps half of everything he earns out of this place for a nice strip of land. Where that'll be, I don't know, but it'll be someplace where I will hang my hat and die an old man and let somebody else fight over the land once I'm gone. Maybe someone else will find their peace of mind... Now, I know what you're thinking, senor. You're thinking, Carlos, what's the point of this story of yours? I'll tell you. My point is life takes you to unexpected places if you try. It may be right away or it may be a few years, but you'll find something worth holding onto and when you do, don't let go..."

Lobo smiled. His advice touched him in ways that Captain Sheldon's didn't and it helped. It made him feel a sense of gratitude. He didn't know why. It just did.

"Carlos," began Lobo, "I'd like to buy ya a drink."

"In that case it'll be on the house, senor Lobo," smiled Carlos. "I'll drink whiskey."

Carlos reached under the counter and took out a glass and a half-empty black glass of something that didn't have a label on it. He poured himself a glass and held it up in a toast.

"To you, senor," said Carlos.

"And to you, Carlos," said Lobo.

They laughed and drank. Just as they finished their toast another customer entered the saloon. It was Macready, who was wearing fresh clothes and was clean shaven. He walked up to the bar counter and sat down two seats down from Lobo. Carlos briefly left Lobo and went up to him.

"Good day, senor," greeted Carlos. "What can I get you?"

"What's he drinking?" Macready said pointing at Carlos.

"Mescal, senor."

"Then that's what I'll have."

"*Si, senor.*"

While Carlos served the man his mescal, Lobo studied Macready. At first, he didn't recognize him without his beard and because of the fresh set of duds he was wearing. By the time Carlos gave Macready his drink it clicked to Lobo who he was.

"Say, uh," began Macready, "other than myself have there been any new faces around here the past two days?"

"*Si*, there has, senor," answered Carlos. "Eight new faces. All of them rough-looking men."

Macready went white. He realized what that meant. It meant that the end of the road was around the corner for him and that he wouldn't be able to deliver his letter and map to his daughter in person. He had to find some other way of getting it there. To be sure he inquired further.

"Eight, you say?" said Macready.

"*Si*," said Carlos. "Their leader was as tall as a mountain with the face of a baby, but the eyes... Oh, the eyes of a violent man. Does the senor know this man and his amigos?"

Macready was dazed for a moment, letting all the information sink in before he realized that the bartender had asked him a question.

"Huh?"

"Does the senor know them?"

"Oh, no," said Macready with a tone of voice that was unconvincing to Lobo. "I'm just a curious fellow, that's all. When were they last here?"

"Early this morning, senor," answered Carlos. "They said they had to get ready for the coach. Maybe you'll see them then, eh?"

"Maybe," nodded Macready. "Just maybe I might."

Carlos shot Lobo a side glance that says there was something fishy here and Lobo only nodded in agreement. Lobo also knew that this was the time for him to butt into the discussion.

"It's a long way to Contention, Mr. Macready," said Lobo.

Macready turned to face him, not hearing him at first.

"I'm sorry?" he said. "Did ya say something to me, Mister?"

"I said it's a long way to Contention."

"Yes, it is."

"Ya got any relations there?"

"None at all."

"Mind if I ask what's troubling you, Mr. Macready?"

Macready became edgy all of a sudden. Who was this guy and how did he know his name?

"Why would ya ask that?"

"Mr. Macready, I happen to be one of the men that brought you into the Fort, and forgive me for saying you've been acting very suspiciously."

Macready put up his guard and acted defensive about it.

"Is that so?"

"Save the attitude, Mister," said Lobo bluntly. "I know you're in a jam. Now, someone has been following you and I have an idea it's these eight fellows that Carlos told you about. Quite frankly, you seem scared to death of 'em. I'm not threatening ya or anything. I am just saying that all you have to do is tell me that you're in trouble and I'll take you straight to Colonel Harding. He can provide you with some protection if you require it."

Macready was quiet. For a moment, he considered it, but then where would that leave his daughter?

Nothing.

"You don't have to keep quiet," said Lobo. "Doing so would only put others and yourself at risk."

"You're very forward, Mr.—"

"Lobo," he answered. "Ben Lobo, and I am forward when I am needed to be."

Macready realized that he had better choose his next words wisely with this one. He was sharp.

"I see that you're sincere," said Macready. "Thank you, but I don't need any help."

"Everybody needs help, Mr. Macready."

"Yes, maybe so."

That was when an idea had occurred to Macready. Why not him? He seemed trustworthy enough to him.

"But the only help I need is to get a message to my daughter."

"Your daughter?"

"Yes."

Macready slowly took the envelope containing the map and message inside and held it up in front of him.

"We haven't spoken in a long time and I wanted to say something to her before you know... Before it was too late."

"Why don't you?"

"It's very complicated, Mr. Lobo," said Macready. "I can't actually face her."

"What for?"

"Well, you see, I did something bad to her a long time ago that I don't think she'd ever forgive me for."

"Maybe you should try."

"Oh, no, I can't. I mean, I can live with her never forgiving me. I just can't live if she doesn't hear me out in this letter."

"Mail it to her."

"I can't," said Macready. "I need to be sure that she reads it. Say, you don't think you could give her this letter for me and be sure she reads it, could you?"

"Now, hold on, Mr. Macready, I don't want to get involved in this."

"It's not far," begged Macready. "She lives in a town on the New Mexico-Arizona Territory line called Border Town. Just outside of that town is a fifty-acre ranch called the Lazy C. She lives there with her guardian, a good man by the name of Rex Johnson. It won't be out of the way. Really, it won't."

He was right. It was not really that far off into the territory line. Lobo had heard of the town as well, but he had never been there. He could see enough pain in Macready's eyes to know that he was desperate. At the same time, he couldn't help but feel sorry for the man. Besides, something inside Lobo told him that he should take it. He didn't know what it was or why, he just took it.

"Oh, thank you, Mr. Lobo!" said a grateful Macready. "You don't know how much this means to me."

"Sure, I understand," said Lobo.

Lobo presented his hand, which Macready limply shook.

"Thank you," he said again.

Macready left money for the mescal and left. Carlos wasted no time to take the money and butt in.

"What are you going to do, senor?" he asked.

"Nothing," said Lobo flatly.

Carlos was taken aback.

"But, senor, he gave you the letter."

"I can mail it when I get back to Santa Fe or any time along the way," said Lobo. "That's all that I am going to do for him. If the man doesn't want my help, then I am not going to get involved."

"But, senor—"

"Look, Carlos," bit Lobo. "I know the man is in trouble. I tried to get Colonel Harding to intervene, but all he's doing is sending three men as an escort with the stage to as far as Contention. The worst part of it is that the three men he picked have little to no battle experience. Now those eight men that you said looked pretty rough were from Kansas City. I know that because Sergeant Sullivan questioned them yesterday. It just so happens that Macready is from Kansas City as well. Now, I don't believe in coincidence, but I'd say Macready is running from them. If he wanted my help, he'd have told me who was after him and why, and I'd take him to Colonel Harding right away. He didn't, and there's nothing I can do about it. Besides, who knows who this letter really is for."

"He said it was for his daughter, senor."

"Just because he *says* it is, doesn't mean that it is."

"The senor sounds final about it."

"Yes, the senor is final about it."

"Ok, okay," said Carlos, backing off. "I won't stop you."

"Good."

Two minutes after Macready left the saloon, one man entered the saloon who was in the same position as Lobo, except he was leaving that day.

"Ben," hailed Don Hinckley.

"Don," Lobo greeted him back.

Corporal Donald Hinckley entered the saloon wearing no uniform with a suitcase in hand. Unlike Lobo who was a New Mexico country boy, Hinckley was a California city boy. San Francisco, to be precise. His talents lay at the card tables of cheap saloons, or mining if he was willing to get his hands dirty. He was not a ranch hand.

"Senor Hinckley," greeted Carlos. "I'm glad to see you before you go. Your stage hasn't arrived yet, no?"

"Not for an hour at least," said Hinckley. "That alone gives me enough time for at least one drink."

"Good, good," said Carlos delighted. "What will it be, senor?"

"Whiskey for me."

"No mescal for you, huh?"

"No offense, Carlos," quipped Hinckley. "But I hope to never taste that snake piss again."

"No offense taken, senor," laughed Carlos. "All you Californians prefer your whiskey, but senor Lobo here, being a New Mexico boy like myself, I think is going to miss it once he leaves."

"Carlos, you never cease to annoy me," smiled Lobo.

"*Si*, senor," laughed Carlos. "What would I do around here if I didn't?"

"You don't do too terrible yourself," complimented Lobo.

"*Gracias*, senor."

Carlos served Hinckley a glass of whiskey before leaving the two decommissioned soldiers alone, chuckling as he did.

"So, when do you leave?" asked Hinckley.

"First thing tomorrow morning," said Lobo. "I report to Colonel Harding at seven and by eight I'm riding out to Contention to catch a coach there."

"And you've already signed your release papers?"

"Signed and filed."

"You should be leaving with me on the stage," said Hinckley. "Not riding out in the morning."

"I know, but what can you do?" said Lobo. "Colonel Harding is strict on formalities."

"You got that right," agreed Hinckley. "You know my offer still stands."

"What offer?"

"The offer I made about you and I meeting in Frisco and me showing you how to have a good time," said Hinckley. "You just can't go back to being a ranch hand for some cattle baron off the beaten path. You got to have some excitement at least once in your life, you know. You should come out with me then to Oregon to take advantage of the gold that's being picked out of the ground. It won't be there forever, you know. It's not like more will grow in its place."

Lobo remembered the offer well. Hinckley had offered it to him many times over his time in the Army.

"Who says that's the life that I want?"

"Well, it's the life that I want and the life that I'm going to live," said Hinckley. "First thing I get back, though, I'm going to marry my girl Etta and we're both going out for some gold. Maybe pick up some extra bits in a game of cards. Hell, before you know it we'll be the new King and Queen of the West."

Hinckley took out a gold watch with a chain and opened it for Lobo to see. He had seen it and the picture many times before. Why not one more time?

"There she is, Ben," said Hinckley. "My lovely Etta."

Inside the watch was a picture of a pale faced, long-haired brunette against the lid.

"She's beautiful, Don."

"She's my girl."

He sealed the watch closed and put it back in his pocket. After that, he finished his drink.

"One more, Carlos," said Hinckley.

"*Si*, senor."

Carlos came over and poured Hinckley another glass.

"Thanks, Carlos."

"*De nada*, senor," said Carlos.

"Now, where was I," said Hinckley.

"You were talking about gold," said Lobo. "And why are you talking about gold, like it's there for the picking like grapefruit, when you know as well as I do that it has really slowed down. What living can you expect to make out of scraps, if you even find that?"

"Where's your sense of adventure, Ben?" said Hinckley. "Without taking a risk, you haven't truly lived a full life."

"Okay, Plato," said Lobo. "I wasn't stopping you. Well, if it's what you both want, then I wish you both the best of luck."

"Much obliged," said Hinckley. "The only shameful thing is that you won't be coming with me."

"Well, you won't be taking the stage alone," said Lobo. "That Macready will be tagging along with you."

"I noticed him outside when I was coming in," commented Hinckley. "What do you make of him?"

"Well, you can find out for yourself on the way to Contention," said Lobo. "He strikes me as a drifter trying to run away from his past, but that's something you can't do forever."

"What's this I've been hearing about an escort?"

"Oh, that," said Lobo. "Well, as a precaution, Sergeant Parker and two others will ride along with you guys up to Contention."

"And you were the one to recommend that?"

"Yes, I was."

"Should I be worried?"

"No," assured Lobo. "I wouldn't be. It's just that I got the impression that Macready was hiding something that has got him all rattled up. There were reports the other day of eight strangers walking into Carlos's saloon and asking some questions, but if anything, they were just men running away from a war-torn South. We'll be seeing a lot of them in the coming months passing through."

"I know what ya mean," agreed Hinckley. "During our time at the garrison we've seen some strange polecats pass through here trying to get away from the war that I pretty much missed, if ya don't count Valverde. But none to me were as odd as this Macready. I don't know. There's just something about him that I can't figure."

"Just twenty minutes ago, I was talking to him," said Lobo.

"What did he say?"

"Well, he asked Carlos if any unfamiliar faces had been around lately. Carlos said yeah, and he asked for a description of one in particular."

"What was his reaction?"

"He seemed scared. I asked him if he needed any help, and he insisted no. He then went on a tangent about a long-lost daughter that he left at Border Town some years ago before the war. He had a letter that he wrote that he wanted to be sure got to her personally."

"Is that it in yer hand right there?"

"Yeah."

"What are you going to do with it?"

"I'll get to that," said Lobo. "Anyhow, he told me to go to Border Town and be sure that she got it, and feeling sorry for the guy, I just took it."

"You should open it."

"What for?"

"Could be something important that headquarters should know about."

"I'm not getting any more involved, past this letter."

"You're actually thinking of taking the letter to the lady, aren't you?"

"Hell no," said Lobo. "I'm going to mail it the first chance I get. After that, I wash my hands of this."

Hinckley finished his drink.

"How about another?" asked Hinckley.

"I'll buy you the next one," agreed Lobo, "but from here on out you drink at your own risk. You don't want to get plastered for the trip, or you'll be making the driver stop for multiple trips just to take a leak."

"You should know me well enough to know that I can take my liquor."

"Suit yourself."

"Carlos," called Lobo. "I'm buying the next one for Don."

Carlos came on over and gladly poured the soon-to-be-departed Corporal another drink.

Forty-five minutes later, the stagecoach pulled into the station. It had two men onboard, the driver and his buddy, riding shotgun with a shotgun in hand. They unloaded the incoming mail in two thick bags before loading the outgoing in bags. Afterwards the two passengers got aboard while the driver and his partner watered the horses.

Lobo walked out with Hinckley to the stage, while Macready, already inside, wasted no time to get aboard. Just outside the stage Hinckley turned to Lobo one last time.

"Well, I guess this is goodbye," said Hinckley.

"Yeah," said Lobo. "I guess so."

Hinckley offered his hand, which Lobo shook.

"Take care of yourself, Ben."

"Take care of yourself, Don," said Lobo. "Give that girl a kiss for me."

"I'll do that," laughed Hinckley.

Hinckley got aboard the stage, and while he did that Lobo got a look at Macready inside. He seemed sullen and distant. For a moment Lobo considered saying something to the old man, but he decided against it when he saw that the man's mind was long ago made up.

He turned at the sound of three horses approaching from behind the coach. It was Sergeant Parker and the two volunteers, privates Quinn and Barton. They both seemed all too eager to go along for the trip that would take them away from the Fort. A chill went through the back of Lobo's spine. In other words, a bad feeling. He walked up to them.

"So, you two volunteered for this assignment," said Lobo. "Why am I not surprised?"

"Of course they volunteered," said Parker, not too keen on the assignment. "I'm the only one that didn't have much of a choice on the matter. I would not have volunteered for it if I had that option open to me."

Lobo laughed.

One thing you learn in the Army. Never volunteer for an assignment. Usually, those were the ones that were the armpit jobs.

"Yeah, I hear you right there, Sergeant," said Lobo.

"I also hear you're moving on tomorrow," said Parker. "I just wanted to say good luck to wherever you go from here."

Parker offered his hand, which Lobo shook.

"You don't have much longer yourself, so I hear," said Lobo.

"Five months is a long time for me," said Parker. "If that's your idea of a short time, then you're crazy."

"It'll go by quicker than you realize."

"Sure," said Parker, not believing him.

"Take it easy out there," said Lobo with concern.

"We're just going to Contention," said Parker. "It may be a lot for these two knuckleheads, but if I had my way I'd be drinking away in Carlos's saloon."

Lobo laughed.

"Yeah," said Lobo. "I'm going to miss the mescal."

"I'm not," added Parker.

Lobo laughed.

"Yeah, that stuff can be tiresome for some," said Lobo.

"Well, good luck to you in whatever you do," said Parker.

"Sure," smiled Lobo.

Lobo then turned to Quinn and Barton, both of whom seemed somewhat gloomy to see their favorite sergeant go.

"Well, Sarge," began Quinn. "We're sad to see you go."

"Yeah," agreed Barton. "It just won't be the same without you."

Lobo smiled.

"You two just stay sharp out there and follow Parker's lead," said Lobo. "Stick close to him. Is that understood?"

"Yes, sir," they both replied in unison.

In the rocky hills a short distance away, the St. Luc gang waited and watched. Charlie himself was asleep against a rock while the others were spread out, killing their boredom with a game of cards, with the exception of Doc Smith, who stood behind the rock facing the mailing station and saloon with the binoculars, keeping a sharp eye out.

The moment Doc Smith spotted the approaching stagecoach in the distance, he sounded off.

"Stage is comin'," he called out to the others.

That got their attention away from their game and very quickly they came to join the Doc.

"Wake the boss," ordered Sugar Lee.

Kid Gray went up to Charlie and shook him awake.

"The stage is a comin'," said Kid Gray.

Charlie instantly got up and joined them.

"Doc, give me the binoculars," said Charlie.

"Sure, boss," said Doc passing them down to him.

Upon taking them, he focused in on the stage and followed it into the station. He had a good view of the faces of those waiting outside the station. Instantly, he spotted Macready.

"I see Joel," reported Charlie.

"Is he gettin' onboard?" asked Kid Gray anxiously.

"Yeah," jumped Buckshot Joe.

"Quiet, all of you," barked Charlie. "Just wait a minute. I'm watchin' 'em."

Charlie watched Macready for a long moment while the others waited by anxiously. After a minute he spotted him enter the coach.

"He's on it," reported Charlie.

"Hot damn," jumped Kid Gray.

That was when Charlie spotted the three soldiers on horseback approaching from the rear of the coach.

"It looks like he's not going to be alone," said Charlie.

"Who else do you see?" asked Sugar Lee.

"Looks like another passenger," reported Charlie. "Plus, a three-man escort on horseback."

"Can you tell their rank?" said Sugar Lee.

Charlie focused harder on the binoculars.

"From what I make out a sergeant and two buck privates," said Charlie.

"What do we do?" asked Silent Duke, breaking his silence.

"Yeah, that's what I wanna know," said Killer Bill with gruffness in his voice.

"I reckon this is it, boys," he sneered. "We'll follow 'em from behind for a couple of miles and make our move once we're out of this Yankee-infested region. Saddle up. Oh, and Jack."

"Yes, boss?"

"Get your gun ready," said Charlie. "You'll be using it."

"Yes, sir," smiled One-Eyed Jack with joy.

"Saddle up, boys," said Charlie. "We move out once they do."

Down at the station five minutes later, the stage took off with the three-man escort following behind them. Once they were moving, the St. Luc gang began following from a short distance behind, out of sight. When they were out of earshot and eyesight of the Fort they would cut around to the front and spring their trap then.

Until then all seemed A-okay.

Privates Barton and Quinn couldn't have been happier that they were doing something that took them away from the every-day grind of the Fort for a change. Nevertheless, the California boys took the time to recall how they were *enticed* into the Army, as they would describe it. Parker, meanwhile, would just sit up a few feet ahead of the two buck privates and just shake his head at how naïve they were. It wasn't out of disgust, because he too had once been in their position as well.

Typically, the two privates were accustomed to working with Ben Lobo. But like Lobo, Parker knew that if these boys ever saw a day of combat, their outlook on life would change in a complete 360-degree turn. What got Parker in particular was that at that moment the boys were speaking about what their recruiters told them to expect. The funny thing was, their recruiters told them the same thing they told Parker when he was aching to enlist.

He could remember the false promises the recruiter made to him. A promise of a life of adventure in a faraway land that was still a wilderness to the civilized world. Faraway land? More like dead and barren land. Sometimes he wondered how it was that the Apaches in their own Apacheria were able to survive out in such barren places like the Arizona or New Mexico territories. Then again, times were different before the white man and the buffalo hunter came along, so he was told. The buffalo alone in some parts were supposed to be numerous. Soon in ten years or so they'll be gone, he thought. Once the buffalo hunters saw that the pickings were slim to none, they'd move on to a climate where the buffalo are more numerous. And eventually they too would fade away into a distant memory, as they were out where he was.

What Parker also knew was that the Apache would fight until they were broken. Many of them were still roaming free, and he knew, like Lobo, that with more whites set to come from the war-torn South to either settle in the territory or move on to California, there would be blood. The only difference between him and Ben Lobo was that Parker had no intentions of leaving before it all got started. Parker didn't mind killing Apaches. To him a savage was a savage. There was no difference.

As far as those promises that were given to Quinn and Barton, Parker wasn't surprised. He knew that a recruiter had a quota to meet and they'd say anything to get the most gullible young buck to sign those papers that signed his life over to Uncle Sam. What surprised Parker was that the recruiters didn't have the imagination to change their lying promises as the years went by. No, they figured a young boy is as dumb and brave as any other. All you have to do is tell them a tall tale pulled right out of your hat.

While the soldiers were behind the stage, the driver and his partner riding shotgun with the scatter gun were more alert. To stage driver, L.J., and his occasional partner, Tucker, they were in wild country. Both of them were in the Army and fought at Apache Pass in '62 under Carleton before mustering out to find work in the stagecoach business. They knew full well what one Apache could do to you when on the war path, so for the duration of the ride to Contention they were in a constant state of alert.

Inside the coach, on the other hand, were two different moods. One was filled with confidence and anticipation, while the other was filled with grimness and regret. Donald Hinckley knew upon entering the coach that he wouldn't have much of a talking companion to lighten the mood, but he was not one to let things like that bring him down. Nevertheless, the silence between them got to him after a while, Hinckley being an extroverted individual. So, he decided to try his hand at small talk with the man in an very different mood.

"So, what takes you to Contention, Mr. Macready?" asked Hinckley.

Macready was instantly taken aback by the fact that the young man knew his name and put up his defensive front.

"I'm sorry," said Macready with caution in his voice. "How do you know my name?"

If Hinckley was nervous, he didn't show it.

"I was a soldier at the garrison," explained Hinckley. "Everyone there knows who you are. The story was that you were on your way to Contention when you had your misfortune. Is that true?"

Macready eased up on his defensive front and gradually began to lighten up a bit. What harm could come to him from a young man like Hinckley? He wasn't even armed.

"Well, no," said Macready. "I wasn't aiming for Contention specifically. I was just going to any place that I could get to."

"So, you're just drifting about, then?"

"You can say that."

"Do you have any family out here in the Territory?"

"A daughter," he answered. "She'd be about your age by now. I'm sorry, I didn't get your name?"

"Oh, I'm sorry," apologized Hinckley. "My name's Hinckley. Don Hinckley. I'm from San Francisco. That's in California."

"Is that where you're heading right now?"

"Well, I'm working my way there," said Hinckley. "It will just take some time to get there with the way travel is out here. There not being a railroad yet and all."

"I see," said Macready. "You got a girl waiting for you?"

Hinckley lit up when he asked and took out his pocket watch and opened it to show him the picture of his Etta.

"That I do, sir," he said. "Her name's Etta."

Macready politely looked at the photo.

"She's pretty."

"Yeah, she is that," said Hinckley putting his watch back in his pocket. "We're going to try our hand at mining for a while. Probably in Oregon. That's where most of the stuff is picked now."

"I once heard that the Alaskan Yukon might be rich in gold," said Macready.

"Is that that big strip of land up north owned by the Russian Czar?"

"Yeah, that's the one," said Macready. "Don't ask me about it though. I've never been there. I just knew an immigrant that was from that part of the region. He came to the States before the war like everybody else and he got caught up in it."

"I think everybody of age was caught up in the war in some shape or form."

"True," said Macready in agreement. "You're awful young. Did you see any of the fighting that was out here? Like Valverde, for instance?"

"Nope," said Hinckley. "The Army had other plans for us California boys; we pretty much have been the ones patrolling this damn territory in case the Apaches decide to go on the warpath, but I haven't seen a single blasted Apache since I first got here. They did so three years ago, but I wasn't around then. No, sir, it's been pretty much quiet since then."

"I see."

"Did you fight in the war?"

"I did some things for the losing side," said Macready. "After Vicksburg, me and some former associates of mine called it quits and came out West."

"You were at Vicksburg?"

"No," Macready shook his head. "Vicksburg was just when we decided to call it quits. By then we had an idea of who was going to win the war and we weren't on the winning side."

"Well, if you don't mind me asking, what did you do in the war?"

Macready laughed. It was an uncomfortable laugh. One that put Hinckley on notice right away.

"I'm sorry," said Hinckley. "I didn't mean to put you on the spot."

"No, it's okay," said Macready. "I'm not afraid to talk about it anymore. I was a Missouri bushwhacker. We did raids on supply lines, hit-and-run stuff on regiments, and held up a couple of trains."

Hinckley was really on the spot now. Not only did he regret asking the old man what he had done in the war, as far as he was concerned what men like Macready did wasn't soldiering, but savagery. Macready could see that was what he was probably thinking, but he did not care. He stopped caring a long time ago.

"I'm not making you uncomfortable, am I, sonny?"

"Oh, no," lied Hinckley. "Not at all, it's just that this is the first time that I've talked with someone from the other side."

That part was a half-truth.

"What made you decide to call it quits?" asked Hinckley.

For a long moment Macready looked at Hinckley. It was a pause that for a moment scared him. The pause was intended to scare him.

"Two things," said Macready, breaking the pause. "The first thing is, there comes a moment amidst all the insanity of the whole war that you have to ask yourself, is all this worth it? Is this cause worth the sake of our lives? We asked ourselves that and we realized that life would go on whether our side won or not, so no. It wasn't worth the risk."

"And what was the other thing?"

"Payment," said Macready. "No fight is worth coming out of empty-handed."

After that Hinckley didn't say much to Macready.

Macready himself was fine with that too, for he had grown weary of the conversation.

Shortly after L.J. the stagecoach driver saw something up ahead.

"There's somebody up ahead," said L.J.

"I see 'em," said Tucker. "It looks like they're in trouble."

"Should we stop?" asked L.J.

"Stop slowly," advised Tucker. "But keep your eyes on 'em."

"Right."

Up ahead the stage, four men were stopped with their horses. One man was lying on his back like he was hurt, and the others waved the stage down. Slowly, the stage came to a stop in front of them.

"What seems to be the trouble?" asked L.J. "Somebody hurt?"

A short distance behind, Parker noticed the stage was slowing down and became alert.

"Quiet, you two!" yelled Parker, interrupting their conversation. "The stage is slowing down."

"Someone up ahead?" asked Quinn.

By then the stage was completely stopped and the three soldiers picked up the pace to catch up, but before they got there an explosion took off on the right side of Parker's head, knocking him off his horse dead.

It was a shot.

Quinn and Barton attempted to come to a stop, but by then it was too late. They were both shot off their horses.

They were dead before they hit the ground.

Hinckley was the first one to notice that the stage was coming to a stop.

"We're stopping," he said. "Why're we stopping?"

"Quiet," said an alert Macready, trying to listen to the driver outside up front.

"What seems to be the trouble," he heard the driver ask. "Somebody hurt?"

Behind them three shots followed. Up front two shots followed with the sound of two bodies falling off the stage.

"Oh, my God," panicked Hinckley. "Is it Apaches?"

Hinckley's answer came with two men stepping up to the stage doors, one on each side, to point guns at the two passengers. Their faces were all too familiar to Macready.

"Hello, Joel," smiled Doc.

"You know these two," said Hinckley to Macready.

"Damn straight he does," said Doc. "Don't ya, Joel?"

"Shut up, Doc," said Sugar Lee.

"What the hell are you two whiskey dicks doin'?" came the voice of Charlie. "Get their asses outside."

"Right, boss," answered Sugar Lee. "All right, you two. I want each of you to stick your hands out where we can see them and step out nice and slow, now."

The passengers did was they were instructed, while both Sugar Lee and Doc with their available hands opened the doors for them. Once they were outside, they got behind each of them to stick their guns in their backs.

"Forward, up front," ordered Sugar Lee. "Keep those hands up high."

Up the front of the stagecoach the two passengers walked with their hands high, walking over the two dead men that now belonged to the dust. Past the bodies and past the horses waited the baby-faced Charlie St. Luc, who was more than pleased to see Joel Macready.

"Hello, Joel," he smiled. "It pleases me very much to see you again, on the one hand. On the other... Not so much."

Macready didn't say anything. He just stood there along with a scared Hinckley, with their hands up in the air.

"Oh, you can both put your hands down now," said Charlie casually. "As for the other man, I haven't had the pleasure. You are?"

"Hinckley," swallowed Hinckley. "Don Hinckley."

"Well, Mr. Hinckley," began Charlie. "Your disposition is that of one who is at the wrong place at the wrong time."

"I'm just trying to get home, mister," said Hinckley cordially. "Whatever business you got here with Mr. Macready is your affair, not mine. Now, if you'll let me walk to Contention, I'll let you do your business with this gentleman. As far as my story goes, we were held up, the coach taken, and I got separated from the others. I don't know your name. I don't know any of your men and I can keep it that way."

Charlie stood quietly looking at Hinckley for a moment as if absorbing his words. For a moment, Hinckley reasoned with himself he was dealing with a reasonable man who was willing to agree to Hinckley's terms, which sparked some hope in him.

"You're going to walk twelve miles to Contention through this Apache territory without a weapon," stated Charlie. "I noticed you lacked your weapon as well, Joel. Did you toss it before the Yankees got you?"

"After I lost my horse, it was a matter of maintaining steady weight while trekking through this desert Hell," explained Macready. "I tossed it along the way."

"A pity we didn't catch you before the Yankees found you," said Charlie with disappointment in his voice. "I was concerned that you wouldn't put up a good fight."

"Sorry to have disappointed you," said Macready sarcastically.

"Indeed," agreed Charlie.

He then turned his attention back to Hinckley.

"Now, getting back to you, Mr. Hinckley," said Charlie. "Yes, I think you are being very sensible; however, I don't think you'd fare well out in this desert on foot, especially without a weapon, but I am willin' to give you a chance."

"How so?" asked Hinckley somewhat eager.

Charlie took out a revolver, a Colt .45 to be precise, and opened it up to take out five of the bullets, which he pocketed before closing the gun.

"In that giant land of the Czars they got this game called roulette," said Charlie. "Are you familiar with it?"

"No," shook Hinckley, who did not like the sound of it.

"It's a rather simple game, really," began Charlie. "You take five bullets out of the gun, leavin' one inside. You take usually two men, have them point the gun at their own heads and pull the trigger. You then pass the gun down to the next man, who does the same thing and this process continues until one of them is dead."

Hinckley was taken aback.

"How can you play such a game?" said Hinckley.

"Oh, believe me," said Charlie with a smile. "We Missouri boys didn't play the game ourselves. We made our Yankee prisoners play it and took bets."

Hinckley swallowed hard.

When the St. Luc gang operated in Missouri, whenever they came across homesteaders, train passengers, or even Yankee soldiers they'd make them play it. When there was an attractive daughter among the homesteaders, they'd force the father and his wife or one of the other children to play it. If they refused, Charlie would allow his men to have their way with the daughter before their very eyes. After they'd make them play the game and one of them was dead, they'd still rape the daughter before leaving a broken family behind with all their money and supplies taken for themselves.

They forced the train passengers to play or they'd die. The Yankees just for the fun and spite of it, since some groups of them would do the same thing to their friends and relations whenever they were raided.

War, you could say, has a way of bringing out the worst in a man.

"You mean you're going to have me play this game with Macready?" stammered a frightened Hinckley.

"Oh, no," shook Charlie. "I wouldn't dream of you playing it with Joel. You're going to play it all by yourself."

"And if I refuse?"

That was when Charlie took out another loaded Colt .45 and pointed it right at Hinckley's chest.

"Then I shoot you right here and the buzzards will eat you away for scraps," said Charlie flatly. "The choice is yours."

"All right," shook Hinckley. "All right, damn you. I'll play your game."

"You hear that, boys," said Charlie to his men. "We're going to have ourselves a show."

His men cheered with savage glee.

Charlie then handed Hinckley the first revolver. The men around got into laughing spirits as they watched Hinckley slowly point the gun at his head. He froze. His whole body shook.

"Cock it," instructed the leader.

Hinckley did as he was told.

"Now pull the trigger," instructed Charlie.

Hinckley could not do it. His whole body shook and his breathing became erratic.

"Pull the trigger," repeated Charlie.

Hinckley still could not do it. Charlie pointed his second revolver right between Hinckley's eyes.

"Pull that trigger or I'll put one right in your noggin' right now," threatened Charlie.

Hinckley could hear his heart beating like it was going to explode.

"One..."

Hinckley could not do it, but he had to.

"Two..."

Click.

Relief went through him.

"Now, was that so hard?" smiled Charlie lowering his gun. "Continue..."

Hinckley cocked it. His whole body shook again.

"Do I have to point my gun at your head again?" asked Charlie.

Click.

Relief went through Hinckley once more.

"That's better," smiled the leader, "only one more time."

Hinckley cocked it. Once again, his whole body shook.

Click.

Hinckley wanted to pass out. He never felt so relieved in all his life. Charlie and his men clapped in applause.

"Very good," said Charlie complimenting Hinckley. "You did very well, now once more."

"What?" said a shocked Hinckley.

"You heard me," said Charlie. "I said again."

"But you said three shots."

"If a man is a degenerate, thievin' murderer, then it is likely that he is a degenerate liar as well," stated Charlie. "Continue..."

Hinckley could not do it. This time he really could not do it. He realized that this man wanted him dead, and he would have to keep doing it until he was dead. Feeling like he had nothing to lose, he pointed the gun right at Charlie's head.

Click...Click...Click...

No bullets. Hinckley looked into the man's face and saw a smile that terrified him. It was the smile of the devil.

"You didn't think I'd give you a loaded gun, now did you?" said Charlie. "Oh well. We've played with you long enough."

Hinckley was dead before he hit the ground, after taking it in the head at the hand of Charlie St. Luc.

It was then that all the attention was turned to Macready.

"Joel, you and I are going to have a nice, long talk," said Charlie.

The next day couldn't have come any sooner to Ben Lobo. He had the option of waiting for the next stage to arrive for Contention, but he wanted to leave awfully bad. He'd had enough of the Army life and the killing that came with it. He'd work his way to Santa Fe in the New Mexico Territory, where he was originally from, and find work as a ranch hand or as a lawman. Whichever of the two came first.

So, Lobo purchased a horse, a Colt .45 with thirty rounds of ammo at a bargain price with a gun belt, a week's worth of rations, and was out of the Fort before noon to forever put his Army career behind him. He followed the stage route from Apache Pass to Contention. He would celebrate the end of his soldiering days with a shave, bath, and a steak meal with a bottle of whiskey. All he could think about along the way was that steak meal he would enjoy. As far as after that, he would worry about it when it came along.

He was not one to fret too much about the future.

For the moment he was happy to be out of the Army, but his joy was only momentary when in the distance from him he spotted what looked like buzzards circling about around the air. He froze on his horse. The buzzards were flying low over the rocky horizon about fifty yards from him. That could mean many things, he reasoned to himself. But he was smart enough to know that it spelled only one thing:

Trouble with a capital T.

"Damn."

He knew what he had to do, so he got off his horse and walked some ways up to secure its reins near some cacti. Lobo then proceeded up the rocky terrain slowly to stop at the top to look down.

"Oh my God," he gasped.

It was the stage from yesterday.

He then rushed back to his horse to ride into the scene of a ghastly crime.

The whole scene was a bloody nightmare. The stage sat in the middle of the rough, sandy road with even the horses dead from being shot.

He came across the bodies of the three soldiers first. They were all dead. From studying the scene, it looked as though a sniper had taken them out from the rocks. Poor bastards didn't stand a chance. Up ahead the driver and the man who rode shotgun were dead from gunshot wounds to their heads, with their bodies decomposing from sitting out in the hot sun. The buzzards were all around them, slowly picking away at their decomposing bodies, and the stench of the whole scene was nauseating to Lobo. It was a smell that he had smelt before at both Valverde and Apache Pass, the stench of death. It was something you would never forget, but wish you'd never smell again.

What got him most of all was the body of his friend Don Hinckley five feet from the stage. Lobo searched his body but could not find the gold pocket watch that had a picture of his darling Etta. He then took a moment to study his body.

It wasn't Apaches. That much was certain. For one thing their scalps were intact, which could have meant anything since most Apaches don't take scalps. What ruled them out to Lobo was that the horses were dead. They would have taken them instead. No, this was someone else's work who had a twisted mind with no human decency, he reasoned. Yet, there was something missing—

"Macready," he remembered.

Where was Macready? He was on the stage too, where was he? That was when Lobo spotted him.

"Oh my God."

Lobo took off running towards him.

Macready lay sprung out against a rock, his limbs outstretched and tied down. His clothes were shredded to his long johns and his body was beaten to a bloody pulp. If anything, he might as well have been dead.

After untying him, Lobo got him to the shadiest spot where he nurse-fed him water. All the while he was in and out of consciousness. Soon after he set a fire, with whatever he could find on the ground. Once he had the fire steady, he focused his attention on burying the bodies.

It took him an hour to bury the bodies. Once the bodies were buried, he returned his attention back to Macready. He had him bundled in a blanket, but as far as the wounds from his beatings went, there was little that he could do. By then Macready was back into consciousness, which was fine for Lobo. That meant he could start asking some questions that he wanted answered.

"All right, Macready," said Lobo. "You better start talking. For starters, who did this?"

"Do you have the letter?" asked Macready weakly.

"Is that what this is all about," spat Lobo as he took it out of his jacket pocket and began to open it, "a Goddamn letter to your estranged daughter or whoever?"

Lobo pulled out the contents of the letter and found two pieces of paper. One a letter, which he began to read and the other was a hand-drawn map.

Upon reading it Lobo looked at the weary, beaten man.

"I don't know whether to kill you or leave you to die," said a disgusted Lobo.

"Please," struggled Macready. "Hear me out."

"No, you hear me out you son of a bitch," barked Lobo. "Because of you, six men and some good horses are dead. I knew most of those men. Two of them were friends of mine!"

Lobo paced around the fire, kicking up sand and dirt as he moved. He was angry at Macready, whom he blamed for the death of his friends.

"That man you rode with on the stage," said Lobo. "He had a girl! He was going to marry her when he got back to Frisco. He had dreams!"

"Instead of yelling at me, maybe you should shut up and listen to what I have to say," said Macready, who was using a lot of energy just to talk. "You can make this right. Just hear me out."

Lobo stopped pacing and looked at Macready with a cold gaze.

"All right," he said, giving in. "But you better start talking. Starting with who killed my friends?"

The letter, which gave a motive to the insanity, was only a piece of the puzzle compared to what Macready told Lobo for the next hour. Macready, according to the letter, was a bad father who had not only abandoned his young daughter upon his wife's death, but something more. He was a Missouri trouble-shooter who was associated with every shady person clear across the South land involved with money-grabbing schemes. He was, most importantly of all, a man filled with regret over the errors of his ways, which had led him astray. In his face Lobo could see a man who was broken on the inside. A man who was dead in spirit, and there was nothing worse than that.

Lobo also found out a lot about the men who were after Macready. They were Confederate bushwhackers turned outlaws. How Macready got associated with them, he didn't say, but it probably had to do with his ability to crack open a safe, which made him pretty handy for whatever pet causes they could come up with to justify their actions. At first, they lived by the Southern cause that was now lost, but after a while they were smart enough to learn that they were fighting for the losing side. So instead of going turncoat, they plundered for themselves.

They stole from banks and ranchers like the bandits they were, but they mostly robbed the supply trains that fed the hand of their losing Southern brothers. It was from one of these trains that they struck the mother lode. The mother lode was two hundred thousand dollars in gold coin. They were also smart enough to know that it was not a loss that their Southern brothers would take lightly, so they hightailed it out of there and went to Mexico.

It was in Mexico that Macready gave them the slip and took the gold with him. When he realized that they were after him, he hid the money and went on the run in the hopes of losing their tail and reuniting with his daughter with the gold. It was a dream that didn't pan out too well.

Charlie St. Luc was the leader of Macready's rough bunch. Macready's description of the man was all too vivid to put a picture into Lobo's mind. Tall as a mountain, with piercing blue eyes that looked right through you, and a gun hand as quick and swift as the hand of God. His description might as well have been the devil's description. As far as the other seven members were concerned, Macready didn't say much about them. Only that they were pretty much followers who looked up to Charlie as their guiding compass. If you killed him, they would go astray, so it was assumed. Any other details about them Macready left out, because he was starting to slip away from the world of the living.

"...I have to be quick," Macready coughed, struggling to remain conscious. "I don't have much time. There is a way for you to make this right."

"I'm listening," said Lobo.

"Chances are likely they will go after my daughter Jill to get the gold. If you can beat them to her, you can take her the map, tell her all that I've told you, and you can both split the gold. You can even take some shares to your friend's next of kin..."

Macready was slipping.

"Will you do it...?"

"I'll take the map to her and tell her everything," said Lobo. "That much I promise you."

"Thank...you..."

"Quickly though," said Lobo. "You said you last left your daughter at a ranch in the outskirts of Border Town? Who owns the ranch?"

"Rex Johnson..." struggled Macready. "If she's not there... He'll tell you where she is..."

With that last breath, Macready died.

"Oh, hell," swore Lobo. "What am I getting myself into?"

It was almost dark, so he decided to make camp there for the night. He buried Macready and tried to get some sleep, but he couldn't.

Macready's words repeated in his head, keeping him awake and staring at the stars. Twice he reread the letter for the estranged daughter Macready wanted to badly to reconnect with. The words stuck out to him.

Now, what are you going to do, he thought to himself. *Once you deliver the map and letter, then what?*

Lobo thought of this Charlie St. Luc and his rough bunch. If he ran into them, things could get rough. He might even get killed. Lobo had given his word to Macready, but he did not want to die. Sure, two hundred thousand dollars in gold was more than enough to last him a lifetime, even a share of that, but it wasn't worth risking his life. He reasoned that he would do the bare minimum in this case. Drop off the map and letter. Tell Macready's daughter Jill everything and then move on to his original destination.

That seemed simple enough.

Jill Macready was a simple girl who enjoyed nothing more than a simple life. Ever since her father left before her twelfth birthday after the death of her mother, she quickly accepted that she would probably never see him again.

Luckily, she wasn't alone.

Rex Johnson, the owner of the Lazy C Ranch just outside of Border Town, who her father worked for, took her in like she was his own daughter. He didn't have any problems about it and neither did she.

It wasn't long before she was like a little sister to his two older sons, who would go on to fight in the war that came and never come back. One died at Shiloh, while the other rotted to death in Andersonville. Out front to the side of the house there were two empty grave spots next to their mother, who had died shortly after the second brother was born.

Those days right after the war it was just Jill, her adopted father Rex, and his two ranch hands, Deke Larson and Fred Cook, who went back to the Mexican war with her adopted father. They had over fifty head of cattle and over twenty horses, it was becoming expensive to keep the cattle and horses alive through a drought that had lasted six months. Then there was talk of a railroad coming through Border Town with the war now over, it was only a matter of time before the railroad would show up.

What was on Rex Johnson's and Jill Macready's mind about the railroad were the possibilities. It would either make or break them.

Her mother's grave was on the other side of the house, by itself. Jill frequently visited it to put fresh flowers on it.

That day was no exception.

It was early morning and she put some fresh daisies upon the grave and said a prayer. Once she was done with her prayer, she found the man that should have been her father standing in the short distance watching her. For a second, he startled her.

"I'm sorry, Jill," said Rex Johnson apologetically. "I did not mean to startle you."

"No, no, you didn't startle me," she said quickly. "I don't know what it is, but lately I've just had the shakes."

"How long has that been going on for?"

"About a week."

"Any idea of what's causing it?"

"No."

"Jill."

"What?"

"You know," said Johnson with tact and affection. "You get this way every year at this time."

Jill knew he was right, of course, for it was the anniversary of when her mother had died and shortly afterwards her father had left her.

"I don't think about him," she said.

"You don't have to lie to me," he said soothingly. "I know it's hard for you."

"But I'm not lying," she said with half sincerity. "Or at least I don't think I am."

"You know nothing will change how I feel about you," he said, "but I am not your father."

"In flesh maybe not," she said quickly.

"He could come back someday, you know."

"He won't," she said with certainty.

"What makes you so sure of that?"

"I don't know," she said. "It's just a feeling that I got."

"Tell me about it."

"Well, I've always known inside since day one that he wouldn't come back," she said. "But that doesn't mean he didn't want to. He wouldn't come back then because he was a coward."

"Was?"

"There's something new to my feelings now," she explained. "He's dead. I don't know how, but I just know he recently died. Maybe in the past day or so."

"What makes you say that?"

"I felt him," she said. "I felt him in my sleep last night. He was in pain over leaving me."

"You think he got caught up in the war?"

"If he stayed in Missouri all this time then he got caught up in it," she said. "Just reading the Washington papers of how bad it was over there, I just knew he would get caught up in it."

"You've been reading the papers a lot this past few years," he said. "Sometimes you read the same one over and over again. I don't want you doing that anymore. All it does is work you up unnecessarily."

"You don't have to worry about it anymore," she said with assurance. "I won't be reading a newspaper for a long time now that the war is officially over. It's taken enough from us both."

Johnson nodded in agreement, while holding back tears. In the corner of his eye he looked at the two empty graves that were meant for his sons that would not be coming home. Two empty graves next to the grave of his dear, departed wife.

"I just got word from Jeff Parker's foreman a short time ago that some of his cattle have been picked up by rustlers," he reported.

"You want me to go do an inventory of our stock with Deke and Fred?" she asked.

"Not just an inventory," said Johnson. "I want 'em rounded up and brought here. Deke and Fred are on their way up the pass to begin. Take my rifle and join them. They shouldn't be too far."

"I'll do that," she said.

"I'll join you in a little bit," he said. "There's some things around here that I have to tend to first beforehand."

"You need my help around here before I go?"

"No, no." He shook his head. "It's nothing like that. I'll catch up in a little bit."

"Okay."

"See you in a bit."

"See you then."

Border Town was in the middle of a sandy valley with a marker in the middle of the town to mark between the two territories of the southeast. To Lobo, it was not much different from Bisbee or Contention or any other town out in the southwest Like any other town, it was just a series of buildings, bleached of color from the winds of the terrain that consisted of the town's structures. The town's faded sign outside pretty much summed it all up to him clear as day.

WELCOME TO
BORDER TOWN
EST. 1857
POP. 580

It summed it up to Lobo as the middle of nowhere in a nowhere land forgotten by God.

To him, it seemed like the town's glory days were in its past and its future was to fade away in obscurity. Not that there was much of either to begin with. Its name would become meaningless once both territories were eventually joined with the Union, which was a matter of years away, he reasoned to himself. Now that the war in the South was over, they would shift their eyes westward for expansion.

The town's only hotel was the first building to the left across the territory line. First thing Lobo would do before inquiring about the Johnson place was secure himself lodging. He thought about reporting to the Marshall about the stage, but that would only raise more questions towards his direction. Such as why did he come to Border Town instead of heading straight to Contention, which was not as far as where it had happened? He also figured that chances were the Fort knew about the stage not making it by then, and in a short while they'd find the seven graves and the remains of the horses with the stagecoach itself. Besides, if he reported it, he didn't know how he could avoid spilling about the gold when he went directly to Border Town instead of Contention.

For better or worse, Lobo had given his word to Macready that he would deliver his letter and map to his daughter. If she wanted the gold, then that would be up to her. Once he delivered the message he would wash his hands of the matter.

The clerk at the desk inside the hotel was an obese man with nothing better to do than read his Bible at the desk. His face lit up upon Lobo's arrival, which told Lobo that business was really slow in those parts.

"Good afternoon, sir," greeted the clerk, putting down his Bible.

"Good afternoon," returned Lobo. "I'd like a room, please."

"Certainly, sir," said the clerk, grabbing the register from below him and placing it open before Lobo. The page was blank. He then took out a pencil and handed it to Lobo for him to sign in.

"Sign here or make your mark, please," said the clerk.

Since Lobo could read and write thanks to his schoolteacher mother, he signed his name.

"How long will you be staying in town, sir," asked the clerk.

"A day at least," said Lobo. "Maybe two. It depends."

The clerk handed Lobo a key.

"Room 17, sir."

"Thank you."

"You're very welcome, sir."

He walked upstairs and let himself inside the room. It was a narrow room with a single window looking down on the territorial line. Against the wall was an iron bed that extended to the right side of the window. Opposite the bed was a dresser that had a wash basin and pitcher on top. Lobo took a moment to study the room.

"Cozy," he surmised.

Not long afterwards Lobo went back downstairs. The clerk sat behind the desk, still reading his Bible. Upon spotting Lobo, he looked up and gave him his full attention.

"Do you know where I can find Rex Johnson's place," Lobo asked the clerk.

"You mean the Lazy C ranch?"

"If that's where Rex Johnson is then, yes," said Lobo.

"I do know where it is," said the clerk. "What business have you got with him?"

"I got a message for him from an old friend," stated Lobo.

The clerk studied him for a moment with a suspicious eye. Lobo thought he should provide more detail.

"It concerns Jill Macready," said Lobo. "That's if she's still there. You see, her father died a short time ago and was unable to return. I'm just here to deliver the news."

"Sam Macready was a troubled man," said the clerk into thin air.

"His name was Joel," smiled Lobo. "And I think you know that."

The clerk smiled back with a little blush in his cheeks.

"Yes, I do," said the clerk with ease. "I just had to be sure that you weren't trouble."

"I understand," nodded Lobo. "If it makes you feel any better, you can fetch the Marshall if you like and have him take it from here. After the War Between the States and the Apaches you can't be too sure."

"No, you can't," agreed the clerk. "All right, I suppose you're okay. Just head on out on the New Mexico side. Once you're out of town, turn east and in a mile, you'll start running into some cattle. That means you're on Johnson's land. Anyway, about a mile in is the Johnson ranch house. If he's not there, then he's somewhere in his land tending to his cattle. Just wait for him then until he returns."

"Thank you."

"You're very welcome, sir," smiled the clerk. "I hope you get there all right."

Like what the clerk had said, Lobo came upon the first sign of the cattle a mile out. He was on Johnson's land, the Lazy C. It was mostly arid with a few waterholes every so often that quenched the cattle's thirst. Rainbow and fire-barrel cactus were spread out across the land, along with patches of grass that the cattle fed on.

Lobo took the time to study the land while trotting along on his horse. For the first time he began to respect the land for what it was. Not that there wasn't anything different than Santa Fe, but for what it was it was beautiful. It had a life to it that touched Lobo to his core. There was something free about the openness of it. It made him feel like he was home.

He liked the feeling. It felt good.

Rex Johnson may not have been a rich man, but to everyone in Border Town he was their richest resident with the biggest spread. There was just one problem. He was not rich enough for the railroad and he never would be. Rumors of surveyors excavating the territory were all over town. The basis of the rumors was that the railroad would be coming to Border Town. Whether or not that was a good thing remained to be seen.

Nevertheless, the rumors scared the townspeople just as much as it had scared Johnson, but he was smart enough to know that he had time.

The very fact that the nation was through tearing each other apart back east meant that the government would turn westward to expand its manifest destiny. Sure, the South would begin to rebuild; but that would take money, and the war took all the money out of the South. The only way money was going to be brought in was going to be through the enterprising opportunities that were abundant out West.

Johnson had been alive enough to read the direction of the wind and it would move by railroad. Yes, with the railroad it would create kings and queens alike in the West. It would also break kings and queens into paupers if they were in the railroad's way. Closer to the time of its arrival, he would know where he stood. Either way, king or pauper, he would be ready. To be ready he needed to take stock of what he had of value. How much time did he have? That he couldn't know for sure, but at the very least a year. At the most, a decade.

He would be ready before then. Personally, despite rumors among town, he had not seen any surveyors and as long as he did not see them, he would be fine. That was until he had spotted a lone rider in the distance. He spotted him as he was outside his home chopping wood for tonight's fire. The rider slowly came in with his back to the sun. Johnson held his hand up to shade his eyes for a better look.

He began to wonder if he was a railroad surveyor, which would mean more would follow. As the rider got closer, Johnson recognized that he was a stranger to town. He was not fancily dressed and not fair-skinned, which ruled out the railroad, so what did he want?

"Are you Johnson?" asked the rider as he approached.

"I am," responded Johnson. "Who are you?"

"My name's Ben Lobo," said the rider. "Is a Jill Macready around?"

"What is she to you?" asked Johnson.

"I got a message from her father. May I have a word?"

Johnson should have known that this day would someday come.

"Where is he?"

"He's dead," said Lobo. "I buried him two days ago just outside of Fort Bowie."

"Why don't you come inside," said Johnson. "You can water your horse and I'll fix you a drink if you like."

"Much obliged."

For the next half hour Johnson listened to Lobo's story. His story of how Jill's father arrived at Fort Bowie half dead, only to die a few days later in Lobo's company with six others dead. He even read the letter.

"I'm sorry you got involved in this, Mr. Lobo," said Johnson with sincerity. "And I am sorry about those other men as well. It's such a damn waste."

"There's more, I'm afraid," said Lobo.

"What more is there?"

"This."

Lobo passed him the map, which he studied for a moment. According to the map the gold was buried half-a-day's ride from the Lazy C in Desperation Canyon. In particular, the third water hole inside. No one went over there unless they had a death wish, for it was on the border of wild Apache country. Anyone going there would only meet their maker the hard way.

Johnson had only one question.

"Where do you stand in all this?"

"Honestly, I want nothing to do with any of it," said Lobo. "I only came here because I gave my word to a dying man I would, and to warn you of the potential danger from these bushwhackers. If you want to go on a treasure hunt that's your business; but it'll take you towards the edge of Apache country, which is where I would rather not be because I've tangled with them before."

"Apache Pass?"

"And Valverde."

"You did mention you were until recently a soldier. I never doubted that. You have the look of one who's seen combat."

"And the rest of my story?"

"I believe it," said Johnson. "For one, I'd recognize Joel's handwriting from anywhere."

"And the other?"

"A man's intuition," said Johnson.

His intuition told him to trust him as well.

"I respect your position, Mr. Lobo," said Johnson. "However, I would like you to stay the evening to tell Jill when she returns. She's out rounding up our cattle with my two cowhands. She should be back before dark."

"Very well," agreed Lobo. "I'll do that."

"In the meantime, make yourself at home."

Jill Macready loved the land she called home. To her it was her retreat from her troubles whenever things got gloomy. Whether it was the loss of her mother, the two boys that should have been her brothers, or the memories of her real father, it was her retreat. She loved working it. It was her home.

After four hours of rounding up fifty head of cattle and spotting over twenty horses, they decided to take what they had back to the ranch house and make another trip out in the evening. She and the two cowhands would sleep out on the range for the night, like many other nights before them. For it was long, hard work on a ranch.

It was just before dark when they approached the house.

"There's a new horse out front," said Deke Larson as they approached the house.

"We got a visitor, I reckon," stated Fred Harper. "I hope it's no railroad surveyor. There have been talk of them nosing around."

"I doubt that," said Jill with certainty. "They always travel in pairs, from what I hear. It's probably just somebody from town."

"That's not the sheriff's horse, that's for sure," said Deke.

Fred said to Deke playfully:

"Still have an eye for the sheriff's horse, huh, Deke?"

"Yep," smiled Deke.

"I figured as much," said Fred.

Jill couldn't help but get a strange feeling about the nature of their visitor. She had to know.

"Can you fellows take it from here?"

"What's wrong?" asked Fred.

"I'm going to check on Pa," said Jill. "He did say he was going to meet us out there, and he didn't."

"You need us to come too?" asked Deke.

"No, I'll be okay," she said.

"Right," said Fred.

Jill went up to the ranch house, leaving Deke and Fred to take what they brought into the corral. She rode up to the front of the house, got off, and tied her horse next to the new horse.

She walked right into the house to find her adopted father in a conversation with a stranger. Upon entering, they both stood to meet her.

"Jill..." said Johnson in a serious tone.

"What's wrong, Pa?"

"This is Mr. Ben Lobo," he said. "Mr. Lobo has a story he needs you to hear. Please sit down."

They all sat down at the dining room table.

"I'm afraid I come with some sad tidings," said Lobo.

"Is it about my father?"

"I'm afraid so," said Lobo.

"Tell me everything," she said. "I want to know."

It didn't take long for the story to be told.

"And that's all of it," concluded Lobo.

Jill sat there quietly absorbing it all in while re-reading her father's letter and glancing at the map. As far as her father went, she was sorry over how it ended and the man he had become. As far as the gold went, she could have cared less. To her it was what got him killed in the first place, why bring that upon herself?

"The gold's yours if you want it," said Jill. "You can send a share to your friend Hinckley's girl. It's the least you can do."

Lobo wasn't surprised that she didn't want the gold. Ever since he first saw her there was a simplicity that told him she wasn't materialistic. A quality that he found rare in a woman. In a way she reminded him of his own mother, which drew him to her. At the same time, he felt that she couldn't understand the potential danger she was in through the St. Luc gang. As long as she had that map, she would be a target, but he didn't want the map either. Between Valverde and Apache Pass, he could see that there were some things not wasting one's life over. No matter the promise it provided.

"I don't think you understand the danger you could be in," said Lobo.

Johnson, knowing Jill, agreed with him.

"He's right, Jill," he said. "It doesn't matter if you have the map or not. If they are aware of your existence, which according to Mr. Lobo they are, they will come here next to find the map."

"I don't want it either, Miss Macready," said Lobo. "But you're going to have to do something about that St. Luc gang, because if they come here, whether you have the map or not, they'll kill you."

"What would you have me do then, Mr. Lobo?" she asked.

Lobo paused for a moment to consider it.

"You well acquainted with the local sheriff of these parts?"

"We are," answered Jill.

"Start with him," said Lobo. "If he's a good sheriff then he'll contact Fort Bowie and put it in the hands of the Army. If not... I'll be in town at the hotel where you can reach me."

Lobo arose from his seat.

"Either way, let me know," said Lobo.

"You're leaving," said Jill, rising.

"I've taken enough of your time," he said.

Johnson got up as well.

"It's almost dark," said Lobo. "I'd like to be back at the hotel before then if possible."

"Of course," nodded Johnson. "We'll walk you out."

As Jill and her adopted father walked Lobo out the door, there were a lot of things on Jill's mind that very moment. Her father was an obvious one, but it was mostly Ben Lobo. There was a quality to him that she had found appealing. It was a world-weary honesty that said a lot.

She liked him. She wasn't happy to see him to leave. As he walked out to his horse and took off, she watched him leave. When he was a mile away, Johnson spoke.

"Help Deke and Fred before you tell them."

"What are you going to do?"

"I want you to spend the night out on the range with them as planned," he said. "You still have work to do."

"You're not joining us?"

"No," he said. "I'll be at the house tonight. I want you to hold onto the map and letter tonight. In the morning first thing, I'll go into town to see the sheriff."

"What will you tell him?"

"I'm not going to tell him anything until I'm sure that he can be trusted. If he says the wrong things, I'll meet Lobo at the hotel and we'll both send word out to Fort Bowie and let the Army deal with it like he suggested. In the meantime, I want you to carry on like nothing's happened. Do your work."

"Sure, Pa."

"Are you okay?"

"Yeah," she said. "I'll be fine."

It was a lie.

Back at the hotel in town, the clerk who checked Lobo into his room was rejoicing at the coming shift change. That was until eight men entered the lobby. Eight strangers who looked and smelt of filth who were very rough-looking. Men on a mission.

"Can I help you gentlemen?"

"Yes," said one who was as tall as a mountain with piercing blue eyes. "We're looking for a man named Rex Johnson. Do you know him?"

"Are you railroad surveyors?" asked the clerk suspiciously.

"Now, sir, if we were with the railroad, wouldn't we be more properly dressed," said the man with a twinkle in his eye.

"Yeah, I suppose you would be," laughed the clerk, flattered. "Are you gentlemen associated with the other gentleman from earlier?"

"What other gentleman?" asked the man, the smile fading rom his face. "Who are you talking about?"

"Why, there was a gentleman here earlier asking about Johnson. I gave him a room and directed him to his place."

"What room?"

The clerk could see he had mis-stepped with his words.

"Now, if you're not associated with him, then I don't see—"

The clerk came to a stop mid-sentence when the tall man took out his pistol and pointed it right at him.

"I'm only going to ask you once more," he said sadistically. "What room?"

"Seven... Seventeen," stuttered the clerk.

"Who is he?"

The clerk had to look at the register in front of him to remember.

"His name's Lobo," stuttered the clerk. "Ben Lobo."

"Never heard of 'em," said the man. He turned to his friends.

"What about you boys?" he asked them. "Any of you heard of 'em?"

"No, boss." They shook their heads.

"That settles it, then," he said turning back to the clerk. "What's your name?"

"Herb... Herbie," stuttered the clerk.

"Well, Herbie," said the man. "Two of my boys here are going to wait with you upstairs in this Lobo's room just in case he happens to show up while we're gone. Have you ever played Russian roulette?"

"No, sir," said Herbie. "I've never even heard of it."

"Oh, it's a fine game," smiled the man. "You'll love it. In fact, it's what you're going to play when I get back. How does that sound to you?"

"That sounds fine, I guess."

"Good," smiled the man. "Oh, and where can I find this Johnson?"

It was dark by the time Lobo got back to town. He wanted to go back to his hotel room more than anything and sleep, but first he had to have a drink. He was craving some liquor.

Right next door to the hotel was a saloon. He was through the bat-wing doors and stepped onto the creaky wooden floor of the saloon and looked around. It wasn't far more extravagant than the saloon back at the Butterfield mail station on Apache Pass, but it was more spacious and seemed more like home. The walls were decorated with bull horns and stuffed animal heads that seemed out of place for any of the animals out in the territory. Crowd-wise, there were three men and a dealer at a card table in the corner and three other men sitting spread out across the room alone with their thoughts and drinks. The bar was empty and the bartender was a short, curly-haired man who watched Lobo with a strange eye.

Upon spotting the bartender's watchful eyes, Lobo went up to the bar to give his order.

"What'll it be?"

"Whiskey."

The bartender poured Lobo a glass.

"You're not from around these parts, are you?"

"No, I'm not," said Lobo taking a sip of his drink.

"You're not from the railroad, are you?"

"No, I'm not," said Lobo. "I've been getting that one a lot around here."

"Well, word has been getting around that they'll be coming through here," explained the bartender. "Word also has it that a few surveyors have been around these parts."

"Won't the railroad help you folks out?"

"Not for some of us, no," said the bartender. "Sure, it'll bring some fresh life and sufficient transportation here, but some of us will be forced to make way."

"What about Rex Johnson?"

"Well, what about him?"

"I just saw him," said Lobo. "What do you think?"

"Well, slick," said the bartender, "that would depend on Rex himself, I suppose. He's got the cattle and horses to turn him a pretty penny, should he decide to sell out. If the railroad doesn't go directly through his land then he could stand to make out well using it to transport his cattle more efficiently. Then again, Rex has been through enough burying his wife and two boys. He could call it quits. Or he might duke it out for Jill Macready, who might as well be his daughter. Then again..."

"Fifty-fifty?"

"Yeah," the bartender nodded after a beat. "That about sums it up."

Lobo finished his drink.

"Care for another?"

"Hit me up."

"You got it, slick."

Next door upstairs in hotel room seventeen, Herbie the clerk was scared. His arms and legs were tied to the bed inside, while two of the eight men waited with him. Buckshot Joe kept the shotgun on the clerk as he sat in the chair by the window. The other, Silent Duke being not so silent, paced across the room impatiently. The stench between the two of them put together made the room reek and Herbie was nauseous as he lay there. More than anything, he wanted to throw up.

"I still can't understand why the boss made us wait here," complained Duke. "I mean he always makes us stay for something, while the others go for the action. With all the times Kid Gray's been running his mouth, you'd think—"

"If you scrubbed under your arms a little better when you take a bath then maybe he wouldn't make you stay with me," quipped Joe. "Quite frankly, I'm getting awful sick of the smell of you."

"Oh, yeah, and what does that make you, the biggest smartass in the whole outfit?"

"You do know that I'm the one with the shotgun, right?"

"Hell, I can draw on you quicker than you can point that thing at me to shoot."

"You're full of big talk," balked Joe from the chair. "Why don't we see if you're a man of action as well."

"You'd wish," said Duke. "Killin' me would mean more of the loot for you."

"That's right," smiled Joe. "It would."

"Mister, I'd feel a lot better if you'd untie me," said Herbie. "I won't go nowhere."

"The next word that comes out of your mouth better be something Shakespearian," said Joe savagely, "otherwise it'll be carved on your tombstone on the hill of boots."

"Quiet," snapped Duke. "I hear someone comin'."

Everyone was dead silent. Outside they could hear footsteps approaching down the hall.

"Remember," whispered the one in the chair at Herbie. "Not a sound outta you."

Herbie thought he was going to piss his pants. He knew the guy was serious. One sound out of him and he knew he was dead. He watched the door as they did. Duke stood by the door real quiet, taking out his pistol and pointing it at the door.

The footsteps got closer until they came to a stop at the door. Herbie froze. It was Lobo. He knew they were going to kill him once Lobo entered or that their boss, the one with the eyes, would. He couldn't help but imagine what he meant by Russian roulette. Whatever that was, he reasoned it might not be good. Either way, the situation wasn't good for him since they already had him.

But what about Lobo? They hadn't gotten him yet. Why should both of them die?

"Run," he shouted.

He was killed by a shotgun blast not a second later.

Lobo wasn't drunk.

After three drinks he decided to call it quits and why not? Originally, he had hoped he could ride out in the morning, but he had to volunteer to stick around until Johnson had spoken with the local law. However, as he thought about it, he realized that since members of the Army were dead and until recently he was in the Army, this meant he was officially involved whether he liked it or not. He knew why he did it, though, and he hated himself for it.

Jill Macready, the golden-haired beauty of Border Town. She would make any man fall over. Then again, there was the gold.

Two hundred thousand dollars was more than enough to last him a lifetime, way more. Even with just a small percentage of that he would be set. For the first time he was tempted. What tempted him were the thoughts of where he came from. His father was a ranch hand Vaquero and his mother was a white schoolteacher. No land of his own and no money. In another way of saying it, he was dirt poor. What was there for him to go back to in Santa Fe? If he didn't find work as a lawman it was off to the big ranches as a hired hand for the big guys...

He didn't want that for himself. Then again, he didn't want to stay in the Army, where all he'd do was kill Apaches, which was what the Army was going to do if they weren't driving them on a reservation like San Carlos. Then again, if he had stuck it out for twenty without losing his scalp, he would have a pension.

Yes, while he sat at the bar in the saloon, he beat himself senselessly over the life decisions of the past few weeks. He had to stop himself, because he was getting emotional.

"Jesus, Ben," he said to himself. "Quit it or you're gonna drink yourself to death."

He paid the bartender and left the bar to head back to his room at the hotel. While he walked, he still couldn't get the situation off his mind. He was particularly wondering if he was going to see Colonel Harding again.

"Evening," he said to the new guy at the desk.

"Evening, sir," said the new guy, who was a tall Black man in his thirties.

"I see you're in for the night shift," said Lobo.

"Yeah, but strangely enough, Herbie wasn't here when I got here. He took off early."

"That's odd," said Lobo.

"I agree," said the night clerk. "You have a good night, sir."

"Same to you," said Lobo.

He walked past the clerk and slowly went up the stairs, thinking nothing of the day clerk leaving early. He was approaching the door to his room when he was alerted suddenly to a shout from his room.

"*Run!*"

It sounded like the day clerk to Lobo. His thought was short-lived when the sound of a shotgun blast followed. Lobo backed away from the door, taking out his Colt as he did. Two shots from a Colt followed through the door before the door opened and a short, rough-faced man in a raggedly outfit stepped out into the hallway. He instantly spotted Lobo and was going to lift his gun to at him to shoot. Lobo didn't hesitate and brought the man down in the hallway with a single shot to the chest.

"Duke," yelled someone from the room. "You son of a bitch! You shot Duke!"

Quickly, Lobo backed off down the hallway by the stairs for cover.

"What in Sam Hill is going on," came the clerk's voice from downstairs.

"Get the sheriff," barked Lobo. "There are some men trying to kill me."

The night clerk ran off to fetch the sheriff, leaving Lobo alone to fight his battle. Down the hall the second gunman barely stuck out of the doorway with his Colt to return fire.

"You're a dead man," he yelled between his shots. "Hey, are you Lobo?"

"What's it to you?"

"You were in with Macready, now weren't you," he spat. "Tryin' to steal what's rightfully ours, aren't you?"

That was when it all clicked to Lobo. This man was from the St. Luc gang. That meant only one thing. The others were heading out to the Lazy C. He had to take care of this polecat and then hightail it back to the Lazy C.

"Where's your friends?" asked Lobo between shots.

"They're on their way to see Joel's daughter, which is a tough break for her."

Finally, the clerk returned with the sheriff, a short, bearded old man who joined Lobo's side by the stairs for cover.

"What's going on here?"

"Two men, maybe three in my room," said Lobo. "As soon as I got to the door they started blastin'. I think they've got a hostage in there."

"Who do they have as a hostage?"

"I think the day clerk."

"You mean Herbie?"

"Yeah, him. I think they killed him."

"Those rotten bastards," spat the sheriff.

"I killed one of them," said Lobo. "There could just be one left."

"One way to find out," said the sheriff. "Hey, you up there."

"What the hell ya' want," spat the gunman, holding his fire.

"I'm Sheriff Brady. Is your hostage alive?"

"And what if he isn't?"

The sheriff shook his head in disgust.

"Then mister, you're up shit creek. Pretty soon you'll be out of ammo and the young feller and I got more than plenty to go around. So, you might as well give up now and make it easier on yourself."

A second later they heard the sound of a rifle followed by a window breaking. They could hear the gunman swearing to himself from the inside and the sheriff couldn't help but smile.

"You still alive, mister?" asked the sheriff.

"Yep," came a hoarse response.

"My deputy has got you covered down below. Try to make another move to the window and he might not miss a second time."

"What if I were to tell you it was Duke who shot the clerk?" came the gunman with desperation in his voice. "What if I didn't kill 'em?"

"Then you'll do a long stretch in Yuma," said the sheriff bluntly. "That's assuming you can prove you didn't kill Herbie, which I wouldn't count on. Especially since you woke me up from a nap. Oh, and there's not a trail of bodies behind you that you're not wanted for."

From the stairs they could hear him curse to himself, repeating a four-letter word that started with an S and ended with a T.

"Make up your mind now, mister," said the sheriff. "Don't make me come in after you, 'cause if I do then you're a dead feller for sure."

Not another word was exchanged. For a moment all was silent until one bullet was fired inside the room, which followed with a loud thump.

Slowly, Lobo and the sheriff got up and walked up to the scene, stepping over the dead man in the hallway. On the count of three they peeked inside. The second gunman was dead. He had shot himself in the head.

"Cowardly son of a bitch," said the sheriff with disgust. "He couldn't take it like a man."

While the sheriff checked the other man in the hall, Lobo stepped into the room and instantly froze.

"Sheriff."

"What is it?"

"Come in here."

The sheriff stepped inside and froze with him.

"My God," he said, taking his hat off.

Before them the day clerk, Herbie, was lying on the bed, tied down with blood everywhere. He was dead from a gunshot wound to the chest.

"When I was walking up to my room, he yelled for me to run," said Lobo. "And they killed him. He died saving my life."

"He knew he was a dead man," said the sheriff. "He figured no point in both of ya' dyin'. He was a brave man."

That was when it came back to him. *Jill Macready, the map, the other six men.*

"Sheriff, we got to get a posse together and ride out to Rex Johnson's place," said Lobo urgently. "I have reason to believe that at least six of these two low-lifes' friends are going after his adopted daughter."

"Jill Macready?"

"I'm afraid so."

"I believe you, son, and we'll do that right now. But you got a story to tell, I reckon."

"I'll explain it on the way."

"Okay."

Night came with a gentle breeze. It was a breeze that felt good against the warm, dry air of the dry climate he inhabited. As usual he was out at his usual spot at sundown. That place was the site of the graves of two sons buried elsewhere, the love of his life, and the mother of the daughter he never had.

As he stood by their graves a lot of things were on his mind. Memories of all the good times he had with his deceased loved ones. But the main topic on his mind happened to be Joel Macready, the man who used to work for him who had brought Jill into his life. He had many questions for him that he knew wouldn't be answered.

Why did you have to leave?

What kind of trouble did you get yourself into?

Why did you have to bring it here?

The railroad was on his mind as well. He was thinking that maybe it would be best to sell the land, cattle, and horses for whatever he could get. He was beginning to think he didn't have the stomach to duke it out with the railroad. Practically losing your whole family can turn you sour on life. He only had one thing left in life worth living for, and that was Jill. Like him, she too had been through a lot. It would take more than a pot of gold to wash away the heartache she had endured. If he could take it all away from her, he would, but there were some things a man just couldn't do. Only time could heal her at that point. Problem is, time can take a lifetime.

"Pa," said Jill from behind him.

Johnson turned around to face her.

"Yes, Jill?"

"We're about to head out," she said. "You can still join us."

"No," he said. "I got to get ready to meet the sheriff in the morning."

"Okay," she said. "I'll see you later then."

Jill turned around to leave.

"Jill, wait."

Jill stopped. She turned around to face the man that should have been her father.

There were a number of things that Johnson had wanted to talk about. Her father for one thing. Ever since Lobo showed up with the note and map, Johnson kept his distance.

"Yes, Pa?"

"There are a number of things that I'd like to say to you, but now it's hard for me to find the words."

"Like my father?"

"Like your father, yes."

"You're my real father," she said. "You were the one who was there for me when Mom died. He just left."

Johnson was touched being called her real father. It meant a lot to him, but he didn't want her to hold any hard feelings about her father, Joel. That has a way of wearing you out before you get to be an old age.

"Jill, I know he didn't do right by you, but I don't want you to hate him."

"It's not hatred that I feel towards him, Pa."

"What is it then?"

"Pity."

"You can't control the things he did," said Johnson. "Once something's been done, it can't be undone."

"I know."

"Have you changed your mind about the gold?"

"No."

"You sure."

"I'm sure," she said. "All it did was kill him in the end."

"I want you to reconsider."

"Why?"

"Jill, please listen to me. The railroad is going to come here sooner or later. When it does the odds are even money that it could go south for us out here. Either way we'll have to be strong, but I don't know if I have the strength to carry on here. I'm broken. My wife and boys are gone and I don't know if I have the strength to carry on should anything happen to you. I want you to think about the gold. Please..."

Jill was in shock. She couldn't believe her ears. She struggled to hide her tears.

"I'm leaving with Deke and Fred," she said.

She turned around and walked away to join Deke and Fred. Johnson made a move to stop her, but didn't at the last second. He didn't want her to see him crying.

In the not too far distance away from Johnson's crumbling world, six riders were approaching. Six riders led by Charlie St. Luc with gold fever and itchy trigger fingers and hearts full of hate.

"What if she ain't got the loot, boss?" asked Kid Gray as they rode.

"I don't expect her to," said Charlie.

"What do ya' mean by that?" pressed the Kid further.

"What I expect is that Joel somehow got word to his daughter," said Charlie. "I don't know how. He just did and we'll have to get it out of her if we have to paint this territory with her own blood to get it."

"Amen to that," laughed One-Eyed Jack.

"But boss, what if she really doesn't know where the loot is," pushed the Kid. "What good is it to be painting the territory with her blood if she doesn't?"

Charlie laughed. It was a sadistic laugh that made the men tremble.

"You fellas are missin' the point," said Charlie. "This ain't just about the loot. It's the damn principle of the matter!"

"Principle," spat the Kid. "What's that?"

"Kid, you may be quick with a gun. But the Lord sure didn't make you the most-brightest one on God's green earth," said Charlie. "We're not just doin' this for the gold. We're doin' this because we can. And we can because we want to. That means we're on the loose, unstoppable. Not even God would dare stop us. We're free men. Free to do what we please, when we please, because that's what this country is all about."

"I say Amen to that," laughed Sugar.

"What if we have to hightail it in a hurry?" said the Kid anxiously. "What about Duke and Joe?"

"They can catch up with us later," said Charlie. "If they can't, then that is their loss and that means more for us, boys!"

All the men broke out laughing at that one.

The night was warm and the sky was bright with the stars. Jill loved nights like these, riding in the night with Deke and Fred. To her these rides drove her closer to the land. Unfortunately, she realized that it might not last much longer. She loved this place, but she also knew that her adopted father didn't have the strength to carry on any further there after all he'd been through. For comfort she remembered what he would say to her when things were at their worst.

"Change is good," he would say, "but change all the time is better."

Sometimes it helped. Sometimes it didn't. That night it didn't.

She was quiet on the ride out with Deke and Fred, but drowned herself in her sorrows on the inside. Deke and Fred, who themselves were quiet, noticed her mood and showed immediate concern. That was another thing that went through her mind. Deke and Fred, Jill had known them as long as her adopted father. They were ranch hands that were a rare breed. They were the loyal type that you called family.

"What's botherin' ya, kid?" asked Deke.

"What makes you think I'm bothered?"

"Knock it off, Jill," said Fred. "We've known you since you were a kid. We can tell when something's botherin' you. So please talk to us."

Jill hesitated a second.

"Dad had some words before I left with you guys," she began.

"About your real father?" asked Fred.

"He was discussed, yes," said Jill. "But that's not what's really bugging me."

"What is it?" asked Deke.

"Dad doesn't think he doesn't have the strength to carry on with the ranch much longer," she said. "Ever since the war he just hasn't been the same. Between losing both his sons and not truly burying them here, he feels broken. It doesn't help that the railroad may end our livelihood here."

Deke and Fred didn't say anything.

"Dad's been thinking a lot about selling everything before the railroad has a chance to get here."

"What else?" asked Deke.

"He wants me to reconsider looking for the gold."

"Oh," said Deke.

"Your father has got a point about the railroad," said Fred. "They ain't a nice bunch to fight with. If anyone's in the way, they'll stop at nothing to clear the way. That's just how they are."

"Did you know about this?" she asked.

"About the possibility of selling out, you mean?" asked Fred.

"Yes."

"He doesn't have to," said Deke.

"We've known for a while that it could happen," said Fred.

"What about my mom?"

"What about her?" asked Deke.

"She's buried on this land. I just can't leave her here."

Deke and Fred sympathized with her. They understand that the idea of leaving a place where one had put down permanent roots would be hard. If they had loved ones buried on this land, they too would be uncomfortable with leaving, but they didn't and Jill did. They understood how emotional it was for her and if they could change that, they would in a heartbeat. But some things you couldn't change. Some things you just had to take as they came along and hoped for the best, and this was one of them.

"Jill, we know it's tough," said Deke. "But you also got to look at this as an opportunity."

"Opportunity," she jumped. "How do you call this an opportunity?"

"What he means is that you got your whole life ahead of you," said Fred. "The war is over now. This Territory going to be added to the Union sooner or later, and that means growth. This country is growin'.

"And with that growth there comes challenges," added Deke.

"Challenges that have to be faced," said Fred. "And the railroad is one of them."

"But why would Pa consider leaving this place?" said Jill with frustration. "The years it took you guys and me to make this place what it is today! Why give it up?"

"He's facing his own set of challenges, Jill," said Fred.

"He's also thinking about you," said Deke. "If the railroad is only going to make things tougher here, then he doesn't want you to deal with that once he's gone."

"Can you understand where he's comin' from?" asked Fred.

"Yeah, I agree," said Deke. "Tell us about that young feller that showed up with the treasure map?"

Jill rolled her eyes in the dark. Ever since she told them earlier about the news of her father and the Confederate gold he stole, they couldn't get enough of the latter.

"Yeah," agreed Fred. "Tell us about that feller. Especially what he told you about the map. In fact, I kinda' like to see it, with me never seein' a treasure map before and all."

"Why not," she said yanking it out of her shirt pocket. "If it'll make you fellows stop talkin' about it."

"It sure would," smiled Fred.

"Yep," seconded Deke.

She handed it to Fred, and Deke lit a match for them to see, and they huddled together on their horses to get a look. They were both quiet for a moment as they studied it.

"Buried under the third waterhole," said Fred studying the map. "That's a half-a-day's ride from here."

"It sure is," agreed Deke.

They both looked up from the map with Jill.

"I'm not interested in stolen gold," she said flatly. "It's blood money."

"That depends how you look at it," said Fred. "That gold has been used to fund the Confederate government, which no longer exists. They're not going to be missing the gold anytime soon or ever."

"You almost sound like Pa," she said. "Before I left, he was lenient towards me going after it."

"Maybe that's not such a bad idea," said Deke.

Suddenly they heard the echo of a gunshot not a distance away that alerted them.

"Was that what I think it was?" said Jill.

"Yes, I'd say it was," said Deke.

Another shot was heard.

"There it goes again," said Fred.

"Sounds like it's comin' from the ranch," said Deke.

"Pa," jumped Jill.

"Slow down," yelled Fred.

Jill ignored them both. Her focus was getting back to the ranch to help her stepfather in whatever trouble he was in.

Johnson finally stopped crying after a while. What good did crying ever do him? It never brought anyone back from the dead. He didn't know how long he stood out there by the graves, must have been a good twenty minutes or so since Jill left with Deke and Fred.

"Got to keep it together," he told himself.

That was when he heard the sound of riders approaching. At first, he thought it was Jill, Deke, and Fred returning, but by the sound of them there were too many of them. Someone from town maybe, he thought to himself.

He looked in the direction that they were coming from and out of the darkness came six strangers. When he saw their faces, he immediately saw that they couldn't be locals. That was when he froze with fear. They encircled him and stopped. He was trapped.

"Evening," said the tallest one in the saddle. "This wouldn't be the Johnson place, would it?"

"I'm Rex Johnson," said Johnson cordially. "What can I do for you?"

"We're looking for Jill Macready," said the tall one.

Johnson knew in an instant that they were the very men that Lobo had warned him about. They were the men that had killed Jill's father and they were there for the map.

"Then you must be Charlie St. Luc," said Johnson boldly.

"Oh, you've heard of us," chuckled Charlie. "Did that stranger what's his name, Lobo, ride in here earlier to tell you all about me and the boys?"

"Among other things," said Johnson.

"Who is this Lobo fellow?" asked Charlie. "How did he get acquainted with old Joel?"

"If you can figure out his name then you can figure out his angle for yourself," said Johnson boldly. "You're a grown man. Figure it out for yourself."

The men broke out laughing.

"The man's got sand, boss," said Sugar.

"I can see that," laughed Charlie. "We can help you, Mr. Johnson, if you let us."

"Then turn around and ride back to where you came from," said Johnson.

The men laughed again.

"He's got some brass balls on 'em, boss," said Kid Gray.

"Knock it off, all of you," said Charlie, losing his patience. "We're here on business."

"I'm going to give you one more chance to make a deal with us," said Charlie seriously. "I warn you, don't trifle with me."

"No, deal, Chuck," said Johnson with finality.

Charlie took a moment to look Johnson over with his eyes. Right away he could tell that he would get no cooperation from him. Johnson himself studied Charlie as well and was thinking pretty quickly.

"You fellows have come a long way from Missouri," said Johnson.

"Yes, we—," began Charlie.

"He's stallin'," jumped Sugar. "Just look at 'em. He's waiting for some company."

"You know what we want, then, I take it," said Charlie, cutting to the chase.

"You're here for the Confederate gold," said Johnson. "I hate to rain on your parade, but it isn't on my land."

"Where is it then?" said Kid Gray anxiously.

"Let me do the talkin', kid," said Charlie.

"I wouldn't know," said Johnson. "The gold isn't mine."

"You got that right," agreed Charlie. "Is your stepdaughter here?"

"She's out," said Johnson. "I can't say when she'll be back."

"Where is she?" repeated Charlie. "You have my word that no harm will come to her as long as you cooperate."

"Do you think I'm really going to tell you damn fools?" said Johnson defiantly.

"Nope," said Charlie unmoved. "I don't think you would."

"Ask him about that fellow, Lobo," said Kid Gray to Charlie anxiously.

"Shut up, fool," spat Charlie.

"He left town," said Johnson. "You missed him."

"Not for long, we won't," said Charlie. "I left two of my friends at his hotel room back in town. When he gets back, they'll take care of him good."

Johnson went for his gun. He barely got it out before Charlie drew his and shot him in the gut, bringing him down on his back in agony.

"Damn it, Sugar, you were right," said Charlie. "The man does got sand. I'll give him that."

"Boss," said Doc, "look."

Charlie looked in the direction that he was pointing. From where the town was they could see eight little lights approaching, getting bigger as they got closer.

"It's a posse," said Charlie. "That fellow must have taken care of Silent Duke and old Buckshot Joe and then got some friends together."

"I reckon they'll be here in a few minutes," said Sugar.

"Yeah," agreed Charlie. "I reckon that."

Charlie turned his attention back to Johnson, who didn't move from where he fell.

"Looks like we'll have no time to play with you," said Charlie. "That's a shame. We could have played ourselves a little roulette. I'll be sure to play that with you stepdaughter, though, before I kill her, after my men have had their fun with her."

"Good luck trying to find her," spat Johnson. "She's too smart for you and that Mr. Lobo you were referring to. If he took care of your two friends that you left for him, then he and the sheriff will take care of the rest of you skunks."

Charlie laughed.

"You can spout all the bullshit you want, Johnson," said a cocky Charlie. "No one will catch us. The Kansas red legs couldn't catch us. The regular Army couldn't catch us. No posse will ever catch us. We got a ride with destiny."

He pointed his gun right at Johnson's head and cocked the hammer.

"As for you," concluded Charlie. "You have a one-way ticket to hell."

"I'll see you there," spat Johnson.

Charlie shot him in the head, instantly killing him. He looked to his men once he was done killing him.

"All right, fellows," he said. "Let's ride."

"What about the girl?" said Bill.

"What about her?" said Charlie.

"Aren't we going to get her?"

"Christ on a horse," spat Charlie. "Do you know where she is, Bill? Because I sure as hell don't, and the way I see it she'll be back to bury her fake father. We'll hide close by in the rocks a mile or so away where we can see the ranch. Wherever she goes, we'll follow."

"What about the posse?" asked One-Eyed Jack.

"If they catch onto our trail, we'll have a nice surprise waiting for them," said Charlie confidently. "Come on. Let's ride."

They galloped away and disappeared into the night, leaving Johnson's body lying by the graves of his family.

Jill double-timed it back to the house with Deke and Fred following behind.

"Jill wait," they called from behind.

Jill ignored them. A few things went through her mind. One of them was a pleading prayer to God.

"Oh, God, please," she prayed to herself. "Not my pa. Please, not my pa."

When she got to the house in half the usual time, she practically jumped off her horse. She scrambled around, looking for Johnson.

"Pa," she called frantically.

She froze when she spotted him lying by the graves. At first, she stood there paralyzed for a moment. During that moment Deke and Fred finally caught up to her and got off their horses. They stopped by Jill when they spotted Johnson as well.

"Stay here, Jill," said Fred.

"No," said Jill.

She walked up to the graves. Fred made a move to stop her, but Deke grabbed him by the shoulder to stop him.

"Let her go, Fred," said Deke.

When Jill got up to Johnson's body, she looked upon his face. She instantly recognized that he was dead. A thousand thoughts went through her head a mile a minute, all of them grief-related.

"No," shook Jill. "No..."

She began to cry.

Deke and Fred stood by in the close distance watching in helplessness. They spotted a group of riders carrying lanterns approaching.

"Look," said Deke.

That was when they recognized the sheriff and the man who rode in earlier. They went up to them as they approached the house.

The posse stopped a few feet away from Jill and sat in their saddles. Jill and Lobo looked at each other, and Lobo didn't like what he saw. That look on Jill's face was a look he had hoped to never see again.

"Sheriff," said Deke as he and Fred approached.

"How long ago did this happen?" asked the sheriff.

"Not long, I reckon," said Fred. "We heard the shots and came riding back. By the time we got back, whoever it was that did it was gone."

"We killed two of 'em back in town," said the sheriff. "They killed Herb, the clerk at the hotel, and tried to ambush Mr. Lobo here."

"They can't be far," said one among the posse eager for the hunt. "We'll get 'em."

"They're bushwhackers," said Lobo. "They won't make it easy for ya to get 'em. They were after Miss Macready. That means they may double back."

"Are you suggesting we wait here and let them get away?" said another with disgust.

"I'm saying one or two of us should stay with them at the house in case they double back," said Lobo.

"He's right," agreed the sheriff.

"No," said another. "We need every man we can get to catch them."

"Then I'll stay," volunteered Lobo. "The rest of you can go. We'll barricade ourselves in the house. If they come back, we'll be ready for them."

"All right," said the sheriff in agreement. "Either way, we'll be back by dawn."

"You get them, Sheriff," said Jill. "You hang them."

"We'll get them, Jill," assured the sheriff. "Don't you worry about that. Let's go, men."

They rode off into the night, leaving Lobo behind with the others. Lobo got off his horse and walked up to Jill.

"I'm sorry, Jill," said Lobo with sympathy.

"We have to bury him," said Jill.

"We will," promised Lobo, "at first light."

"Jill, we have to get inside the house," said Lobo. "If they double back, we'll only be sitting ducks out here."

"He's right," said Deke, stepping forward. "We have to go inside the house where it's safe. Rex would want us to do that."

"But we just can't leave him out here," said Jill.

"He's not going anywhere, Jill," said Deke. "He'll still be here at first light."

Deke put his hand on Jill's shoulder.

"Come on," said Deke. "We have to go inside."

"Okay," nodded Jill.

They went inside.

Meanwhile, the St. Luc gang was setting up a little surprise for the posse.

"Here they come, boss," announced One-Eyed Jack.

"All right," said Charlie. "Pick your targets. Shoot when I shoot."

They were hidden in the rocks about a mile from the house with their rifles, ready for some shooting. The posse was rapidly approaching. As they got closer their targets got more defined.

"Remember, boys," said Charlie. "Aim for their lights. Keep them in the dark."

"Right, boss," said Kid Gray, "Whenever you're ready."

Charlie took aim at the rider in the dead center, aiming for his lantern. He waited.

"A little closer," he thought to himself. "Just a little closer..."

After a minute of careful aiming and waiting he took his shot. He hit the lantern, but it didn't put the lantern out like he thought it would. It ignited it, setting the man and his horse aflame. With that, the whole posse came to a halt as the rest of Charlie's men began to open fire. The men in the posse at least were smart enough to drop their lanterns, which didn't do them much good. Two of them were instantly killed from the shots, while the one that was caught aflame jumped off his horse and tried rolling over to put out the flames. The others returned fire on their horses, but they were shooting blind.

Charlie's men cheered.

"We got them, boss," cheered Bill.

"Look at that one roll over," cheered Kid Gray sadistically.

"Keep shooting, boys," ordered Charlie. "We're licking them."

They continued firing. The light from the full moon provided the bushwhackers enough light to see the posse.

The men in the posse continued to fire, but they found themselves being picked off one at a time. Ultimately, they retreated when there were three of them left. All the others were dead except the one that was on fire. By then the fire was out and his horse was long gone. He couldn't get to his feet, for he was burned badly. All he could do was lie in the sand surrounded by his dead friends and cry in pain.

"Hold your fire," ordered Charlie.

They stopped firing and began cheering again.

"Look at them run," cheered Kid Gray.

"All right," yelled Charlie. "Keep quiet. There's still that one left alive out there."

"Oh, he isn't going any place," said Bill sadistically.

"Maybe," said Charlie. "But we got to make sure him and his friends are dead. Come on now, let's go."

"Right, boss," said Sugar.

Six killers came out of their hiding places to walk fifteen yards out to the bodies.

"Put a bullet in each of the bodies," ordered Charlie. "But leave the one left alive for me."

Slowly they worked their way to the bodies. With their revolvers they each put a round into the bodies. Except that Charlie didn't kill the last one left alive right away.

It was the sheriff.

"Evenin'," said Charlie.

"Damn you," he cursed Charlie. "You go to hell."

"Looks like you've been there before me," said Charlie.

The sheriff couldn't help but laugh.

"Yeah," he said. "Maybe so, but what I got was nothing compared to what you'll get a taste of."

Now it was Charlie's turn to laugh, which he did.

"I've had worse said to me," he said. "Now, I'll cut to the chase. I like you, therefore I want to give you a chance to save your life."

"You don't say," said the sheriff, not believing a word of it. "What do you have in mind?"

"A little game of roulette."

The sheriff laughed. It was the laugh of one who was facing death itself.

"You're laughin'," said Charlie. "You've heard of the game?"

"I've read a book or two."

"Then you'll play?"

"Hell, no," spat the sheriff. "Chances are, you've played this game with others, and how many of 'em did you let go in the end?"

Charlie couldn't help but like the guy. Not only did he have sand, but he had a brain. It was a combination he liked in a man.

"Very true, friend," said Charlie.

"So, you go ahead and kill me," said the sheriff, "because that's what you were going to do in the first place. But know this. You can't do what you do forever. Sooner or later a man like me will step up and hunt you down like a dog. He will show you no mercy."

"Okay, okay," said Charlie. "I get it, but before we get down to brass tacks, I want to know three things. Who is Ben Lobo? Is he among your dead?"

The sheriff laughed. Charlie didn't find it so amusing.

"Now what's so funny?" said Charlie impatiently.

"He's waiting for you with a few good men at Johnson's place. You go there, you'll be stepping into your own grave."

"Like you and these men here," laughed Charlie shaking his head. "No, I don't think so."

"You said three things," said the sheriff. "That was two."

"So, it was," said Charlie. "Where is Joel Macready's kid?"

"You mean Jill?"

"Yeah, I mean her."

"Good luck trying to get her. She's got two ranch hands that are veterans of the Mexican War. Along with 'em and Mr. Lobo, who is a veteran of the War Between the States, they'll give you a good fight."

"Thank you," said Charlie.

"What the hell for?"

"You just gave me the numbers of the men with the girl," said Charlie. "There's only three of them to deal with."

"Four."

"Four?"

"Counting Jill," said the sheriff. "She'll fight you."

Charlie laughed even harder than ever. He didn't see how a girl was a match for him and his men.

"Nice one, friend," said Charlie.

He then shot the sheriff dead with one shot. After that he looked to his men, who were standing around waiting for him to make his next move.

"What next, boss?" asked Sugar.

"Now we head back to the house," said Charlie. "The way I see it, the remains of the posse will be headin' back to town with their tails between their legs."

"Leavin' the girl available for the takin'," said Kid Gray. "I hope she's pretty."

"Exactly," said Charlie. "And you can have first poke at her, Kid."

Kid Gray cheered with excitement.

"Now let's move," said Charlie.

Back at the house, Lobo took the time to tell Deke and Fred what happened back in town. Jill was nearby, dazed and in another world.

"And that's the gist of it," concluded Lobo.

"What about the gold?" said Deke.

"What about it?" said Lobo.

"Did you tell the sheriff about it?" said Fred.

"No, I didn't," said Lobo.

"Why not?" asked Jill from across the room.

"I was going to let you guys do that if you wish," said Lobo. "Or—"

"We go after the gold ourselves," said Jill, finishing Lobo's sentence.

"If that was what you want," said Lobo. "Then yes. It's yours."

"It's the Confederate government's property," said Jill flatly.

"Ok," said Lobo. "But to tell you the truth, I don't think they'll be missing it anytime soon."

"He's right, Jill," said Deke. "They might as well not have existed. It'll all just go to the Union or whoever takes it first."

"Which would be the four of us," said Jill.

"Could be," said Fred. "Or maybe your father's killers, do you want that?"

"Hell, no," said Jill with disgust, "but I still don't want it. As far as I'm concerned, it's yours, Mr. Lobo."

"Now, wait a minute," said Lobo. "If I wanted it for myself, I wouldn't have bothered to come here to bring you the map, remember?"

"I remembered," said Jill.

"As far as I'm concerned, it's blood money," said Lobo. "I don't want anything to do with it."

"Both of you are mighty mixed up," said Fred shaking his head with frustration. "You know—"

"Quiet," interrupted Deke. "Do you hear that?"

It was the sound of approaching riders.

"Douse the lights," said Deke, "quick."

Quickly they blew out the lights and grabbed their rifles to rush to the windows to open them and aim their guns at the dark.

"Is it them?" said Jill with an itchy trigger finger.

"Could be," said Deke. "Don't shoot unless we tell you."

Relief went through them when they saw it was part of the posse, and they lowered their rifles.

"It's the sheriff's group," said Lobo.

"Yeah, but where's the sheriff?" said Jill.

"You in there," called one. "Don't shoot. It's just us."

"Where's the sheriff?" said Deke.

"There is no sheriff," said the one. "Not anymore. It's just us now. They ambushed us."

"Come on in," said Jill. "We'll wait them out."

"Are you kidding," said another, "I'm a bartender, not a gunfighter. I didn't sign up to be shot at like a dog."

"What are you going to do now?" asked Deke.

"We're going back to town," said the third. "What else are we going to do? You're on your own as far as we're concerned."

With that said, they turned around and galloped back to town.

"They just can't leave us here," said Jill, not taking it too well. "Why, they—!"

"You can't blame them," said Lobo. "They just had their asses handed to them."

"He's right, Jill," said Deke.

Jill took a deep breath before speaking.

"In other words, we're on our own, then?" she said.

"I'm afraid so," said Lobo.

"We'll hold out till dawn," said Deke. "If they show up, then we'll be ready for them."

"But we're outgunned—" began Jill.

"We have the defensive position," said Lobo, cutting her off. "That gives us an advantage as long as we stay in the house."

"What about Pa?" she asked.

"He'll still be there in the morning," said Deke. "We can bury him then."

"But—"

"Jill," said Lobo, stepping up. "We're going to be all right here. We just have to keep our wits about us until dawn. Once it's light-out we'll be able to move then. I'm sorry about your pa, but he would want to you to be safe. The only way you're going to be safe is sticking close to us and not losing your head. I know you've been through a lot, but you'll overcome this. That I can promise. Just trust me."

There may not have been any light, but Jill could see an outline of Lobo's face in the moonlight and could see that he was sincere. His sincerity touched her. Again, like earlier when he brought the map, she felt drawn to him. There was a strength in him that reminded her so much of her pa.

"I'll trust you, Mr. Lobo," she said.

"Please," said Lobo, "call me Ben."

"Sure," she smiled. "I'll do that."

The room fell silent for a moment. It was obvious to both Deke and Fred that she liked Ben Lobo, but they were dead quiet. However, despite not wanting to interrupt the chemistry between them, they had questions for the ex-Army sergeant.

"What happened back in town?" asked Deke.

Lobo looked at them, about to answer, but suddenly realized that he couldn't remember their names. Jill could sense that and was the first one to speak up.

"Oh, Ben, this is Deke and Fred," she said. "They've been with Pa since the Mexican War. I told them all that you've told Pa and I."

"Sorry to meet under such circumstances," said Deke modestly. "Is it true that you got two of them back in town?"

"Well, yes and no," said Lobo, shaking his head.

"What happened?" asked Jill.

It took Lobo less than four minutes to get them all caught up on his end. He told them about the hotel clerk back at the hotel in town that died warning him of the trap he was walking into, which saved his own life, but not the clerk's. What he meant when he said yes and no was the fact that he had actually killed just one of them, while the other, when faced with no chance of escape, took his own life.

"Damn skunk," spat Fred. "He got off easy."

"Where were you stationed during the war?" asked Jill eager to know more about him. "You were stationed in the Territory for the duration?"

"I was," answered Lobo.

"Where at were you stationed?" asked Deke.

"Fort Bowie."

"Then you were at Apache Pass in '62," said Fred.

"I was," answered Lobo. "As far as the war with the States goes, the only combat I've been in was at Valverde. Pretty much after that it's been hurry up and wait at the Fort."

"And you left as a sergeant?" said Jill.

"Yes, only a few days ago, in fact," said Lobo.

"Where's home for you?" asked Jill.

"Well, I'm from Santa Fe where my pa worked as a ranch hand, while my mother was a school teacher, but they're both gone now," said Lobo. "I was probably going to head back there and see what I could get as far as work goes before all this."

"Look, I know where you stand on the gold," said Deke to Lobo. "But we could use your help."

"Ben," said Jill, "a few moments ago I could've cared less about happened to that gold. I saw it as blood money like how you do, but then something happened. The last thing my pa said to me before I left with Deke and Fred earlier was that I should consider going after it. Well, seeing my pa dead out there I've made up my mind. I cannot abide his killers getting what my birth father took from them. I am now onboard with Deke and Fred. We're going to take it, but he's right. We need your help. We'll split it four ways. If you find you still don't want your share after all of this is said and done then you could always send your share to your friend Hinckley's girl or to a church or something."

Lobo paused for a moment to think it over. He could decide about taking his share for himself later, but they were right. They needed all the help they could get. Besides, gold or no gold, he couldn't leave a lady to fend for herself in a fix like the one she was in. It wouldn't be honorable.

"I'll help you," said Lobo. "I'll stick with you till the end of this whole thing until it's done or you don't want me anymore, or if I'm killed. As far as my share goes, I'll figure that out after."

It may have been dark, but Lobo could tell that she was smiling at his answer. He smiled too.

"Quiet," said Deke. "Listen."

They all got quiet and listened. Riders were approaching.

"It's them," said Fred.

They all picked up their rifles and quickly got by the open windows up front. In the pale moonlight they could see six riders approaching.

"I'll fire a warning shot," said Deke. "In the meantime, everyone holds tight and don't fire."

"Right," said Lobo.

Deke fired his warning shot above their heads. They stopped approaching at about ten yards and came to a stop.

"That's close enough," called Deke. "What do you want?"

"We're here for the girl."

"You can't have her," said Deke flatly.

"Oh, we don't want her," said the same one. "We want what she has."

"And just what would that be?" said Jill.

"You must be Jill, I take it," said the same one. "I'm Charlie St. Luc. My boys and I have ridden with your pa."

"Until you killed him," said Jill testily.

"Only after he stole what was ours for himself," said Charlie. "It was nothing personal."

"Like what you did to Johnson," spoke up Lobo. "Was that nothing personal?"

"I take it you're the mysterious Ben Lobo," said Charlie.

"I am," replied Lobo.

"What happened to my two friends I left back at the hotel for you?"

"The sheriff and I placed them on the white throne of judgement before the Lord," said Lobo defiantly. "It's where we'll place you and the others if any of you takes one step closer."

"I don't see how this concerns you, Lobo," bit Charlie.

"Oh, it does not, huh?" bit Lobo. "One of the guys you killed at the coach was a friend of mine. He didn't do anything to deserve what he got from you."

"Instead of saying who killed who," said Charlie impatiently. "How about we get to it now, shall we?"

"Speak your piece," said Deke.

"Before we left Joel out to dry," said Charlie, "he spoke of a map he made."

"I don't know what you're talking about," said Jill.

"Don't be cute," said Charlie. "We're not dumb. We know you have it. He buried the gold somewhere in this desert and he left you the map. How? I figure now that he must have given it to you, Lobo, because we were hot on his trail and he didn't come here straight away."

"How did you know to come here?" asked Jill.

"That was simple," laughed Charlie. "Your pa told us."

"You're lying," said Jill in disbelief. "My father was many things, but he wouldn't give me up to a gang of snakes like you."

The rest of Charlie's men broke out laughing with him.

"Am I?" said Charlie. "Now, you just think about this for a second here. If your old man had the nerve to leave you in a place like this, then what would stop him from telling us?"

"It's not like he didn't have much of a choice," added Kid Gray, rubbing it in. "He was a weak man when it came to grit and torture..."

Charlie was about ready to knock Kid Gray off his horse to shut him when...

"All right," jumped Deke savagely. "You've said enough. Now turn around and get out of here."

"We're not going anywhere without that map," said a sinister Killer Bill. "You give it to us, we'll leave you be."

Charlie wanted to reach to his other side next to him and knock-off the head of Killer Bill.

"Damn it, Bill," bit Charlie in a whisper. "Let me..."

"What the hell for," bit Bill. "All you're doin' is just playin' with them. They ain't going to give up the map if you coddle them. Besides, we outnumber them. They can't shoot us all. I say we charge them. They can't shoot us if we all come charging in together..."

"You step any closer and we'll shoot," warned Fred who overheard them.

"Bill..." said Charlie in a sharp tone. "Don't..."

"I'm done listenin' to you and your bullshit," spat Bill. "I'm not waitin' around on you anymore either and neither are the others. Come on, fellows, let's..."

A shot suddenly took Bill right off his horse and brought him dead on the ground. The shot came from Charlie himself and all eyes turned directly to him, who had just shot Bill on the side of his head.

"Is this true about you boys siding with him?" said Charlie sinisterly. "Anybody else want to go against me?"

He turned to Kid Gray next to him and pointed his gun right at his face in the dark of the moonlight.

"How about you, Kid?"

The Kid was shaking in his boots.

"No, boss," stammered Kid Gray. "I'm with you. Hell, you know Bill was the one who was always second-guessing you. Not me. I mean, I got a mouth, but not a mind to outthink you."

"That you don't," laughed Charlie. "How about the rest of you? Let's hear it."

The remaining three men, who consisted of Doc, One-Eyed Jack, and Sugar Lee all said the same thing: "No, boss. We're with you."

"Good," smiled Charlie, turning his attention back to those in the house. "Now, where was I...?"

"You're pretty quick with the trigger," said Lobo. "Kill one more and the odds will be even money against us. Even if you do decide to attack us this moment or any moment in the future, remember this. We have the defensive position and we got enough ammo and supplies to last us a long while. Do you?"

Charlie bit his lip. He knew then that he wasn't going to get anywhere going at them the way he was going. He could also feel the eyes of his remaining men glued to him.

"Sooner or later you got to come out of there," said Charlie. "How else are you going to get the gold? You got to come out of there. When you do we'll make our move then, so the next move is yours to make. I suggest you make a smart move, because it might be your last."

Charlie turned to his men.

"Come on," he said. "There's always another day to fight."

Without saying another word, Charlie turned around and rode off into the dark with his remaining four men following right behind him, taking Killer Bill's horse with them, but leaving his body for the defenders to bury. Once out of sight, the defenders relaxed.

"We probably should have opened fire on them without giving a warning shot," said Fred. "A few more of them might have gotten killed. Hell, if we killed the leader, then the others would be lost without him."

"That crossed my mind," said Deke.

"Then why didn't you do it?" asked Jill.

"Killing a man isn't easy, Jill," explained Lobo. "Once done, a part of you dies with the other fellow. It's a part that you never want to die."

"And that is?" she asked.

"Our innocence, Jill," said Deke. "That's something that you never want to lose."

"Wouldn't it be different killing someone who deserved it though?" she asked.

"No," answered Lobo. "Whether you're in the right or the wrong, when you kill someone you always lose a part of yourself. Once you lose it, there's no getting it back."

"Is that what happens to men in war?" she said. "They go in like a bunch of happy cavaliers, but once the killing starts it's no longer fun?"

"Pretty much," answered Deke.

"What about Charlie St. Luc or whatever his name is out there?" she said. "It may have been dark, but the moon gave enough light for me to see the look on his face when he gunned one of his men down in cold blood like that. A man like that..."

"War does things to a man, Jill," explained Lobo. "It can bring out the best in good men and the worst in bad men. In Charlie St. Luc's case, it brought out the worst."

"He's also unstable," added Fred. "A man like that you can't negotiate with. He will never show any mercy towards us if he ever gets the upper hand. He'll downright kill us in cold blood."

"That's why we're going to have to kill him when the time comes," said Deke.

"Not just him," said Fred. "All of them. It'd be wrong to leave even one of them alive. All they'll do is cause terror until doomsday. We can't let that happen."

"What do you think his next move is going to be, Ben?" asked Jill.

"I think he just told us," said Lobo. "He'll make a move after we make a move. He knows he can't take us on while were shacked up in here. Him and his men have neither the time, supplies, or inclination to come after us while we're here."

"Then we'll wait here for a while, then," said Jill. "A week or two. In less than that they'll be forced to move on out. After what they did to the sheriff and his posse, sure they may be running scared, but it won't take long for them to get up their nerve to reorganize and go out hunting for them again."

"You may be right on that point, Jill," said Lobo, "but we can't afford to wait."

"What do you mean?" she said.

"Think about it, Jill," said Deke. "If more people find out about that gold then the chances of us getting it are pretty slim."

"Deke's right," said Lobo. "If we don't get that gold before more people find out, we won't be able to go after it. The Army will step in for us and take over. These snakes, as you call them, have already killed four Army personnel from my garrison. If we don't get that gold in the next day or two, we will lose control of the situation. And if we lose control then the whole ugly truth comes out."

"Assuming we don't get the gold," said Jill.

"Yes," nodded Lobo. "Assuming we don't."

"If we get it, though, and take care of them then we can tell the Army and the town whatever story we like," said Jill.

"Exactly," said Lobo. "Now, on the ride here I briefly filled in the sheriff about the situation, but I didn't mention the gold. As far as him and that posse knows, the St. Luc gang is just out on a blood feud."

Jill walked over to the table and put her rifle down.

"So, what now?"

"Now we stay up the whole night if we have to and keep watch," said Deke.

"I doubt they'll try anything before the morning," said Fred.

"Only one of us needs to be up to keep watch," said Lobo. "We can sleep in shifts till dawn. I'll take the first shift."

"All right," agreed Deke. "I'll relieve you at one. Fred will relieve me at four, who will take it till sunup."

"What about me?" said Jill. "I should do something."

"You need to sleep," said Deke. "We'll take care of it till dawn. You just keep hold of that map."

"I doubt I'll ever be able to sleep," she said.

"Maybe so," said Deke. "But you have to try."

"Let me at least stay up a while with Ben," she said. "Any objections to that?"

"That's up to Ben," said Fred. "How about it?"

"I have no objections," said Lobo.

"All right then," said Deke. "It's settled then. Fred and I will be at the back of the house."

"Okay," nodded Jill.

"Let's go, Fred," said Deke, already walking.

"I'm coming, Deke," said Fred following behind.

Jill and Lobo were alone then.

"Do you want me to make some coffee?" she offered.

"That'd be mighty nice, thank you," said Lobo.

"Okay," she said, getting to it.

They spent the whole shift alone together, sharing the coffee. It was mostly small talk that was exchanged between them, but before their shift was done, they each found out one thing about the other that they kept to themselves.

They were in love.

A mile away in the cover of the rocks Charlie and his gang waited and watched. Charlie himself was as patient as he was cold and calculated. He knew when to run, when to fight, and when to wait. However, for the first time since killing Bill moments before he was unsure if he could keep his men together much longer.

After all that they'd been through he knew that he couldn't keep them waiting much longer for the gold than necessary. Every man had his limitations and he was smart enough to know that his men were beyond their limits. He figured if he didn't get a win for them in a matter of days then even Sugar Lee would turn on him.

They were all quiet when they went to the cover of the rocks. So was Charlie. He could feel them watching his back, watching and waiting for what could be not much longer. After an hour it was Sugar who broke the silence.

"What's the play, boss?"

Charlie decided to play it assertively.

"We wait and we watch," he said.

There was a quiet among his men for a moment. It was a cold, uncomfortable quiet. It didn't take a moment for Charlie to realize that he had better say something else.

"They'll move out tomorrow," he said.

"How do ya know they won't wait us out?" asked Sugar.

Charlie expected that question from Kid Gray, but not Sugar. How did he know? He didn't. He was following his gut and his gut told him that they couldn't afford to wait either.

"The longer they wait," said Charlie clearly, "the chances grow slim of them being able to get that gold. The rest of that posse we faced off will reorganize and get up the nerve to come after us again. Chances are they're sendin' word to the next town in the territory to the Marshall there and in a matter of days he'll show up with men of his own. Once they do and if they hadn't moved out of that house by then, they will lose their advantage as far as the gold goes. They won't be able to go after it."

"Neither would we," said Sugar.

"But they won't," said Charlie with certainty in his voice.

He turned around to look at them.

"I'll keep first watch," said Charlie. "The rest of you try to get some rest. Sugar, you relieve me at one and take the rest till sunup."

"Right," said Sugar dryly.

His remaining men went about to get some rest, while Charlie turned back to look at the house before them. One thing was for sure, he was not going to sleep that night, even after Sugar would relieve him. Until they got the gold, Charlie was going to have to keep a sharp eye on the rest of his men.

That much he knew.

Dawn finally came without Charlie and the remains of his bunch making a move. Shortly after sunup, with no sign of Charlie anywhere, they finally buried the bodies. One in a marked grave next to the empty graves of his sons who would never come home. The other they placed in a shallow one out back. After saying a few words out of respect, they took out the map and studied it together for the first time.

Between the ranch and hostile Apache territory were three waterholes. Each waterhole was five miles apart. The map indicated that the gold was in a Confederate Army storage box that was at the bottom of waterhole number three. There were just two problems with that. First of all, the third waterhole was at the edge of Apache Territory. No one, except one with a death wish, dared venture beyond that. Second of all, Apaches were believed to use the third waterhole for watering their horses. The chances of them encountering Apaches at the waterhole were high.

For five minutes they pondered the situation. It would be a full day's ride to the third waterhole. If they were lucky, they would make it there before dark. Staying the night there was the scary part. Fred was the one to voice that. The others pondered for a moment before Deke answered for him.

"We'll cross that bridge when we get to it."

Fred also asked about the St. Luc gang. To which Deke again replied:

"We'll cross that bridge when we get to it," he said to add: "Either way, we should pack plenty of guns and ammo."

Lobo said they had better get started before it got deeper into the day so that they would have light when they reached the third waterhole. Without saying anything else they got moving.

In the distant horizon of the Arizona desert, four riders took off with two additional horses in tow. Over a mile behind them were the five riders that consisted of the St. Luc gang. Among the gang, Charlie was finding it difficult to keep the confidence of his remaining men in his leadership, but they only followed out of their lust for gold.

Charlie couldn't help but wonder if he should have just killed the rest of the men and keep at it on his own. To him they were starting to feel like a weight that was only holding him down. At the same time though he was smart enough to know that he needed as many men as he could to overpower his opposing competition for the gold. Plus, there were the Apaches to consider. Charlie was a stranger in that godforsaken Territory. If the desert climate didn't kill him then the Apaches most certainly would, and he hated the idea of facing down a bunch of savage Apaches all by himself.

He did not like that kind of odds.

"Boss, I dunno about this," said Sugar cautiously.

Now Sugar Lee was questioning Charlie. That was the nail in his coffin right there. All that was needed was a hammer to put the nail in. Charlie knew he would have to choose his words carefully with Sugar. Next to him, Sugar was the smartest of who were left.

"What's the problem, Sugar?" said Charlie with assertive concern.

"Less than a day ride from here is Apache Territory," he said. "I'll give Joel one thing, he was smart to hide it out here. Not too many would venture out here unless they were eager to lose their scalps."

"We'll be fine," said Charlie with his best poker face.

"I've heard stories of what those Apaches do to white men, boss," said Kid Gray sounding scared. "It isn't pretty."

"Don't think about that," said Charlie quickly. "Think about all that gold that you're going to get your hands on."

He thought about trying to be funny to lighten the mood.

"And if you're still thinkin' of those damn savages, consider this," he said. "We sure gave those Yankees sweet hell back home, didn't we? Well, think of the sweet hell we'll give them savages should they decide to tangle with us. It sure would be something."

Charlie laughed a little, but no one laughed with him.

None of them were in a laughing mood and that scared Charlie, so he tried something else.

"Look at it this way," he tried. "We're in the finish. It won't be much longer now. That I can tell you."

No response.

Charlie thought then that maybe he should try keeping quiet for a while. Either way he was right on both accounts. Should they encounter the Apaches it would be something, and they were in the finish.

It wasn't long before they saw that they were being followed.

"I think they're following us," said Jill, getting a sore neck from looking back.

"Yeah," confirmed Deke. "They're following us."

"I'd say they're at least a mile behind us," said Fred. "Maybe a little further than that."

"And they'll keep their distance," said Deke.

"What makes you say that, Deke?" asked Jill.

"They won't make a move on us until we got our hands on that gold," said Lobo.

"He's right," agreed Deke. "They don't know where it is. Otherwise they would have killed us already."

"What are we going to do about them?" asked Jill.

"Right now, I don't want you to think about them," said Deke. "You focus on what's ahead. Fred and I will keep an eye on them."

"What about the Apaches?" she asked with concern.

"That's my job," said Lobo. "I'll keep an eye out for them. We're not even at the first waterhole yet. You just keep looking ahead."

Slowly, the day went by. They came to the first two waterholes, where they filled their canteens and watered their horses with no trouble from the St. Luc gang. The gang itself didn't make a move on them. They kept their distance from their prey, but watched them like hawks.

When they came to the watering holes, Charlie himself kept an eye on them through the scope. Once they left the first two watering holes to continue onward, the gang would quickly fill their canteens and water their horses.

They made it to the first waterhole without any trouble. It wasn't until halfway to the third that Lobo first spotted the Apaches.

"Look to your left at ten o'clock," said Lobo. "It's the Apaches."

They looked and saw two Apaches on horseback about a hundred and fifty yards out by the rocks, keeping their eyes on them.

"Well, they've spotted us," said Fred.

"They're only scouts," said Lobo. "They won't touch us until we pass the third waterhole and head right into their territory."

"Or attack 'em," added Fred.

"How much farther is it to the third waterhole?" asked Jill.

"No more than two to three miles, I'd say," answered Deke.

"Once we get our hands on the gold up ahead, the gang will make a move on us," said Lobo. "We better start thinkin' about how were going to handle them."

"He's right," said Fred. "We better start thinkin' of something."

"Any ideas, Ben?" asked Jill.

Lobo looked around their surroundings, thinking sharply. There were a lot of rock formations all around them. It gave them plenty of places to take cover should the gang make their move on them. That was when things began to take shape in Lobo's mind.

"When we get to the waterhole," began Lobo carefully, "Jill, I think you and I should go for a swim."

Jill's face froze. She liked the idea of that, but found it not to be the right place or time to get acquainted-like.

"Not to get acquainted," said Lobo quickly. "To look for the gold. I'll start on one end, you the other, and we'll work our way to each other. We're going to cover every square inch of that waterhole. Deke and Fred will keep a sharp look out, but pretend to water the horses. Once we find the gold and grab it we'll make a run for those rock formations to the right over there, but still have access to the well for water."

"And let Charlie come to us," said Jill getting the picture.

"Exactly," said Lobo. "We'll make him come to us."

"And the Apaches at our backs," said Fred.

"They shouldn't bother us unless we bother them," said Lobo. "But rest assured, they'll be watching us."

"Why do you think that?" asked Jill.

"Your answer is up ahead at your left ten o'clock," said Lobo.

They looked up ahead to their left and saw two Apaches on horseback at about a hundred and fifty yards out by the rocks, keeping an eye on them as they approached.

"What about Charlie and his bunch?" asked Jill. "Will they just ignore them?"

Lobo's face froze for a moment. Yes, that thought had occurred to him, but he didn't want to think too much about it.

"That, Jill, is the hundred-thousand-dollar question," said Lobo.

It wasn't until twenty-five minutes later when Charlie and the remains of his gang spotted the Apache scouts. The scouts were no more than thirty yards from Charlie and his gang, having allowed Lobo's group to pass on ahead.

"Look, boss," said Kid Gray who spotted them first.

"I see them," said Charlie.

"What do we do?" asked Kid Gray.

Charlie thought for a moment before getting a sadistic grin.

"Sugar," he said. "Bring me one alive."

"And the other?"

"Kill 'em," said Charlie. "But bring me his scalp. They actually pay for Apache scalps, so I hear."

"Sure thing, boss," said Sugar with excitement in his voice.

Sugar went charging after the two Apaches with his rifle out. At about twenty yards out he shot the first one dead. The second attempted to flee, but he shot his horse out from under him and the Apache broke his leg on the rocks falling off his horse.

He was all Sugar's.

Charlie and the others just sat there on their horses watching Sugar in action. For the first time since finding Joel there was excitement in them and that brought relief to Charlie. That meant they weren't focused on him.

Up ahead, Lobo and his party stopped and watched the scene in the distance.

"Damn fools," spat Lobo. "They're attacking 'em."

"Don't they know that the Apaches will be on 'em now?" said Fred.

"They'll be on us too," said Deke. "Don't forget, we're white as well. To an Apache a white man is a white man. We better get out of here, and fast. Come on."

Quickly, they turned around and continued on their way, double-timing it to the waterhole, leaving Charlie and his friends to play rough.

After collecting the dead Apache's scalp, Sugar tied a rope around the waist of the wounded Apache that couldn't have been no more than thirteen years old and dragged him on the back of his horse to Charlie and the others. They were all happy to see the Indian. The way they saw it, it would give them an opportunity to play.

"I got 'em, boss," said Sugar.

"Good man," said Charlie.

"I don't see what you could want with 'em though," said Sugar. "He's a plum kid."

"All the better reason to play with 'em," said Kid Gray sadistically. "Right, boss?"

"That's right, Kid," nodded Charlie.

The Apache, worn out and beaten with a broken leg, looked up at Charlie with a defiant look. He began to say something in Apache, which they of course couldn't understand. Not wanting to hear any of it, Charlie took out his gun and shot him in his broken leg.

The Apache stopped his talking to grab his leg and scream in pain. His cries of pain brought pleasure to them.

"All right," said Charlie to the Apache. "Stop your crying. Take it like a man, if that's what you think you are."

The Apache stopped screaming and looked up in Charlie's eyes, filled with rage.

"Damn you," he spat in broken English. "Damn you to hell!"

They laughed, most especially Charlie.

"Oh, he understands you, boss," laughed Kid Gray.

"You speak good American for an Apache," said Charlie. "Did your dad's white squaw you're poking behind his back teach you?"

"Tall white man, play with Apache," said the Apache.

"Yes, tall white man does play with Apache," laughed Charlie. "Tall white man also loves to see Apache suffer."

"Tall white man fight, like how woman fight," spat the Apache.

"Tall white man think Apache should shut up," said Charlie.

"Tall white man should make Apache shut up," he dared.

"Fair enough," said Charlie.

With those words Charlie fired a second shot into the Apache's throat. It didn't kill him, but forced him to shut up. The wound made him bleed internally, which made it feel like he was drowning in his own blood.

"Do we kill 'em, boss?" asked Kid Gray.

"No," said Charlie. "We drag 'em along for a while on the back of our horses. The wounds and the desert air will kill him. He'll just suffer in the meantime. Come on, let's go."

They continued on their journey, pulling the Apache along on the Arizona ground. He was dead within twenty minutes, and he suffered to his last breath.

While Charlie and his men continued on their way in the distance, a third Apache watched. He was much older than the other two, who were practically young bucks. He swore to himself and the spirits of his ancestors that his two young braves would be avenged.

Five minutes in the waterhole told Lobo that they would not find the gold, for it wasn't there. Someone had beaten them to the punch. While doing a doggie paddle, which was the only way he knew how to swim, he told the others. Deke and Fred were watering their horses, but were really keeping their eyes out for the trouble behind them. Jill on the other hand was at the other end of the well pretending to bask in the desert sun.

"You sure?" she asked.

"We would have found it already," said Lobo, somewhat disappointed.

"Well, at least we know Charlie and his bunch won't get it," said Jill. "I'll take pride in the fact that they maybe never will."

"While you're basking in your pride," said Deke, "any thought as to how we're going to deal with the gang of snakes?"

"Us not getting that gold kind of changes things a bit," said Fred.

"Maybe," said Lobo. "Maybe not."

Deke looked at Lobo, who was standing in the well with the water up to his waist, thinking.

"What you thinking?" asked Deke.

It didn't take Charlie five seconds to see that they were looking for something in the waterhole. He wasn't slow to share that information with his men.

"You mean the gold could be there?" said Kid Gray, perking up.

"I mean it must be there," said Charlie, looking through his scope.

They were fifty yards from the waterhole, hiding behind rocks, out of sight. Charlie took a moment to study the area around them.

"What do you figure their play is, boss?" asked Sugar.

"You see those rocks over there on the right by them?" said Charlie.

"Yeah," said Sugar. "I see them."

"The moment they find the gold they'll take it out and make a run for those rocks to wait us out. We can't go around them without being seen by them, which would leave us wide open. If we just waltz on up there straight ahead, they'll pick us off like ducks in a row. They can wait us out with access to the water, but they know that after what we did to those two Apaches, we won't be able to stick around unless we are aching to lose our scalps."

"But we were just having fun, boss," said Kid Gray.

"I know," agreed Charlie. "It was a much-deserved fun, but now it could become a hazard."

"What's the play?" asked Sugar.

"Jack," said Charlie.

"Yep."

"Kill one of 'em."

"Which one?"

"How about we start with the man in the water with Joel's daughter," said Charlie. "Make it a head shot. My gut tells me that one's that Lobo fellow."

"You got it, boss," smiled One-Eyed Jack, looking into the scope of his rifle to aim.

"Now, once—," instructed Charlie.

"Boss..." said Kid Gray.

"Not now, Kid," bit Charlie. "Now..."

"BOSS!"

"WHAT?"

"Behind us."

Charlie turned around and froze. They all did.

Not ten feet behind them were eight Apache warriors armed with bows and rifles all aimed right at them.

"What do we do?" said Sugar with terror in his voice.

The terror in Charlie's face prevented him from answering.

Kid Gray meanwhile made a play for it.

When reaching for his gun an arrow went right in through his chest and out his back. He stood a moment, coughing blood, and looked at Charlie.

"They've killed me, boss... They've..."

A second arrow went through him six inches below where the last arrow hit him. That one sent him on his back, dead.

Doc screamed and raised his shotgun and managed to get a shot fired before taking a rifle round to the stomach, knocking him flat on his back. The round he fired did no damage to the Apache that shot him, but knocked the wind out of him on his rear in such a way that his fellow warriors broke out laughing.

But the moment he got back on his feet they all closed in on the rest of the gang, and Charlie and his remaining men, with nothing to lose, drew on them.

It did not go well for them.

At the first shot they froze. Their attention turned to directly behind them. Immediately they heard the cry of the Apaches and the screaming of the men of the Charlie St. Luc gang.

But they couldn't see them.

"Sounds like the Apaches made their move on them," said Fred.

"Sure does," said Deke.

That was when Lobo felt it in his gut. A feeling that made him freeze dead cold.

"Everybody freeze and keep your hands out in the open," said Lobo with urgency. "Slowly turn around and whatever you do don't react."

Slowly they all did as they were instructed. In front of them were a dozen Apache warriors, no more than five feet from the well and armed to the teeth.

"Anybody speak Apache?" Jill asked.

"A little," said Deke.

"I know Apache for hello," said Fred.

"I speak the lingo," said Lobo.

"Better start talking," said Deke. "Make it good."

"Yeah," said Lobo suddenly feeling the pressure.

Lobo stepped out of the well, and an elder Apache stood forward that had to be the leader.

He began talking. The dialect was broken, but clear. Deke understood enough to get the gist.

"What's he saying to them?" Fred asked Deke.

"If you let me listen, I'll tell you," bit Deke.

Fred let him listen.

"He's saying that we aren't with those polecats that killed their two braves a short while ago," said Deke. "He also adds that they were after them, killed Miss Jill's father and sought to shame her. Blah, Blah, Blah..."

Once Lobo was done talking the elder Apache spoke. He spoke not a minute before a younger, more fierce Apache stepped up to speak in protest.

"Now what?" said Fred.

"Well, the elder that has to be the leader is more understanding," explained Deke. "But that young buck speaking up was close to the young bucks that that wild bunch had butchered. One of them might have been a brother. Real or blood I don't know, but he's challenging Lobo in a fight to the death."

Once the younger Apache was done speaking, the elder nodded in acknowledgement and said a few words that made Deke tremble.

"What now?" asked Fred.

"The leader is saying something to the effect that if we are going to walk out of here with our scalps intact, Lobo will have to fight the young one. If he lives, then we can walk out of here. He's also speaking of the gold."

"What about it?"

"The elder says not to come any further for the white man's gold we seek," said Deke. "He said after the fellow that put it there, they fished it out and took it for themselves. It's their treasure now. The treasure that we should be interested in is our lives, because life is the true treasure."

Disappointment somewhat went through Fred.

"You mean we came all this way for nothin'?"

"Quiet now," said Deke. "What happens now is in God's hands. Let's pray that he's lookin' out for us."

Once the talking was done Lobo turned to Jill, who was still standing in the well.

"Get with the others," he ordered.

"What is it?" she asked.

"Just do it," he bit.

Without saying another word, she quickly went to Deke and Fred.

"What's going on?" she asked.

"Lobo's facing the war knife," said Deke. "If he loses, we lose our lives."

Jill's eyes went glued onto Lobo whose back was to her. She watched as Lobo and the challenger disarmed themselves with the exception of a tomahawk for the Apache and Lobo's own Bowie knife. The rest of the Apaches stood back a few feet, giving the two fighters the necessary space for their fight.

It was over in five seconds: when the Apache came charging, Lobo boldly threw his knife and made a direct hit square in the Indian's chest, stopping him in his tracks. For a moment the Apache stood there in disbelief at the sight of the knife in his own chest before he fell on his back, dead.

Lobo went up to the now dead Indian to remove his knife from the dead man's chest and looked boldly at all the remaining Apaches.

In bold, straight English Lobo said:

"Anybody else feelin' lucky?"

The Apaches were silent for a moment. No one dared challenge him. The elder Apache looked around at his men and could see that before nodding to Lobo.

In straight English the elder Apache said:

"Go now and value your treasure well."

The elder Apache said something to his braves in his native tongue, and two Apaches came forward to take away the body of their foolish dead brother. Upon hitching him on his horse, they all turned around and left the four whites in peace.

Lobo then turned around and faced his friends, who wore looks of surprise.

"Now I know not to mess with you," said Fred.

"I didn't see that coming," said Deke.

"Are you okay?" asked Jill with concern in her eyes.

Lobo looked right at her. He had just killed a man in cold blood and for a second, he was afraid that she would look at him differently, but instead, the look she gave him was the look of not hate or disappointment, but love.

"I'm all right now," answered Lobo. "Let's get out of here."

On the way back Lobo translated and explained to the others what had happened back there, but it was mostly for Jill's benefit. Deke got the hang of it and having already explained it to Fred, it was not necessary. At first there was disappointment that they had come all that way and would only come back empty-handed, but each of them, in their own ways, were relieved.

"What did he mean by treasure?" Jill asked Lobo.

"To an Apache, besides dying well there is nothing more sacred than life," explained Lobo. "The Apaches aren't materialistic in the way that we are."

"But they took the gold," said Fred. "There's some greed in them."

"They don't look at the gold as a means to a new life, though," said Lobo. "They recognize it as a tool we use to better ourselves, but to them they'll use it to get what they need from trading with renegade whites to fight."

"That figures," said Fred.

"At least those renegade whites that followed Joel here are done for," said Deke.

"What a relief that is," agreed Fred.

"So, what now?" Jill asked Lobo.

"Well, I'll have to go back to town and get word back to Fort Bowie and report the situation. The fact that the Apaches have the gold now is something that the Army has to know. That only means there will definitely be some more fighting with them, maybe sooner than I thought. One thing's for sure, it'll be ugly."

"No, I mean about you?" said Jill.

"Me?"

"Yeah."

Lobo was quiet for a moment.

"I don't know," he said.

"Why don't you stick around for a while," said Jill. "With Pa gone we could really use another hand. You'll have a place to hang your hat and whatever we decide to do with the ranch, the cattle, and horses, there will be a piece in it for you."

Deke and Fred looked at each other quietly. They were smart enough not to say anything, but they were sure watching and listening. This was the moment.

Lobo thought about it a moment and smiled.

"All right," said Lobo. "I'll stick around until you have no more use for me."

"Oh, I don't think you have to worry about that," said Fred.

"Fred," bit Deke.

Fred, realizing his error, shut his mouth.

Jill blushed while Lobo laughed.

"No," said Lobo. "I think this is the start of something beautiful, Jill."

"I think so too, Ben," she smiled.

THE END

Don't miss out!

Visit the website below and you can sign up to receive emails whenever Tom Hyland publishes a new book. There's no charge and no obligation.

https://books2read.com/r/B-A-IYAS-CKOWB

BOOKS 2 READ

Connecting independent readers to independent writers.

About the Author

Tom Hyland is an LA native currently living on Hilton Head Island, South Carolina with his folks and canine companion Daisy Mae. A volunteer assistant librarian, a nature photographer, a bibliophile and a cinephile. He is on the autism spectrum.

Read more at allmylinks.com/pulpmastertom.

CPSIA information can be obtained
at www.ICGtesting.com
Printed in the USA
LVHW100439210622
721699LV00005B/99